Grinning In His Mashed Potatoes

MARGARET MOSELEY

BERKLEY PRIME CRIME, NEW YORK

GRINNING IN HIS MASHED POTATOES

A Berkley Prime Crime Book / published by arrangement with the author

PRINTING HISTORY
Berkley Prime Crime edition / August 1999

All rights reserved.
Copyright © 1999 by Margaret Moseley.
This book may not be reproduced in whole or in part, by mimeograph or any other means, without permission. For information address: The Berkley Publishing Group, a division of Penguin Putnam Inc., 375 Hudson Street, New York, New York 10014.

The Penguin Putnam Inc. World Wide Web site address is
http://www.penguinputnam.com

ISBN: 0-425-16982-0

Berkley Prime Crime Books are published
by The Berkley Publishing Group,
a division of Penguin Putnam Inc.,
375 Hudson Street, New York, New York 10014.
The name BERKLEY PRIME CRIME and the BERKLEY PRIME CRIME design are trademarks belonging to Penguin Putnam Inc.

PRINTED IN THE UNITED STATES OF AMERICA

10 9 8 7 6 5 4 3 2 1

"It's about
Twyman Towerie."

I held out my hand with Twyman's very expensive diamond on it. It was easier to wear than stuff in my pocket. Clover gave the ring a sideways glance. "Yes, I've seen that. Twyman showed it to me the night before he died. Tried to give the damned thing to me."

"Then it's yours," I declared, starting to take the ring off my finger.

"Oh, no, you don't. I don't want that thing. Wouldn't take it from him and won't take it from you." She slammed the hat back on her head, shading her best remaining feature from the sun. "I was the damned fool who married him twice. The stupid old fool thought I was up for grabs for a third go round. Told him where he could put that ring," she snorted. "Waited many a year to tell him off. Almost made up for everything. Took me almost a lifetime, but almost made up for . . ."

Her voice trailed off . . .

The Edgar-Nominated Debut Novel
Bonita Faye

"An offbeat whodunit."   —*Publishers Weekly*

"Moseley's characterizations are deep and deceptive . . . Nothing is ever as it first appears . . . Best of all, this author offers a startling fresh voice and a literary original you'll want to share with friends."   —*Tulsa World*

"Ms. Moseley's first novel will remind some readers of *Fried Green Tomatoes* and others of the heroine in *The Burning Bed*."   —*Dallas Morning News*

FOR RONAL*

Acknowledgments

Once upon a long time ago a dear friend taught me about *serendipity*: that magic meeting of chance and good fortune. Now I find myself laughing with the muses as I thank those serendipitous friends who give so sweetly of their time, talent, and friendship to help me with my writing. Margaret Ann and Keith Smith, Ginger and Max Courtney, John Dycus, Miles Hawthorne, Anne Miller, Michelle Tezak, Sandy Wakefield, Bob Watson, and Cassey Browning.

And thanks to those professionals who have become friends: my agent Jake Elwell and my editor Tom Colgan. Also to book owners and managers Lee, Charlie, Bret, Peggy, Geraldine, Amy, Jan, Patsy, and Dean, who tell all their customers about Honey!

Personally I must throw a kiss to my beloved sisters, Donna and Mary Lou, and my darling daughters Dixie and Charlotte. Along with a high-five to Da Sistahs: Doll, Rets, Susus, Debs, Sara, Calli, Gracie, Burry, and Muse, as well as the TWIGS.

Nursery Rhyme

Georgie Porgie, pudding and pie
Kissed the girls and made them cry.
When the boys came out to play
Georgie Porgie ran away.
Author Unknown

One

The second–best-selling author in the world ate his dessert first.

I probably wouldn't have noticed, but I was sitting next to him, and when he took that first bite of the Eagle Brand lemon pie with the mile-high meringue, I wished I had the nerve to do the same.

My mother always said, "Eat your vegetables first," so I did, even though she died more than ten years ago. She might have had a point. Twyman Towerie licked the meringue off his lips with a satisfied grin and fell over dead into his mashed potatoes.

And I lived to tell the tale.

Of course, there was a scream. And, of course, it came from my friend Janie, who was also sitting at the squared head table at the Friends of the Arlington Public Library annual luncheon. Although she is a devoted mystery fan and reads blood and gore without batting a lash, Janie always screams when she sees a dead body. She's working on it, but Towerie's death made her two for two.

Association with death—murder, to be exact—is why Janie and I wound up at the head table usually reserved for authors and their friends. I was recently featured in the Fort Worth *Star-Telegram* as having had two—not one, but two—murders occur in my life. And since I am a book representative for a small, respectable number of publishers, the Friends of the Arlington Public Library naturally assumed that the combination of books, murder, and publicity would help entice more readers to their fund-raiser.

Janie accepted the invitation for me and announced to the chairman over the phone that she would be my lunch partner. She's into books, too. She owns a bookstore, Pages, a converted gas station in West, Texas, which sells all kinds of paperbacks but specializes in mysteries.

Although romances, not mysteries, were my thing, I was actually getting quite good at knowing what to do when one finds a corpse. Or in this case, when sitting next to one.

After my first embarrassed reaction—"Mr. Towerie . . . are you all right?"—I realized he was not and jumped to my feet. Not used to wearing high heels, I had slipped them off under the table. Now my left foot scrambled to find a toehold on the missing shoe while my right one slipped into a slot between the straps. I made an uneven lurch toward the downed author.

I put my hand on his shoulder, and the big gray head rolled off his plate onto the table. That was about as far as my expertise went, and I looked out into the audience and said the numbers that had helped me before: "Nine-one-one. Nine-one-one."

The faces that seemed frozen for the few seconds following Janie's scream suddenly went into overdrive, creating a blurred image of a previously still picture. A few darted off to the hallway, hopefully to call the magic number, and two purposeful bodies strode toward Twyman.

"Doctor."

"Doctor."

I assumed that meant they were doctors, so I stepped aside to let them at him. Of course, that was another lurch, which threw me back into my chair, so I got to see all the resuscitation stuff up close.

The two—a man and a woman—gently laid Twyman on the floor, loosening his tie and belt while opening his shirt. I looked away then, but could hear the pounding swooshing sounds that obviously went with the correct professional behavior in such a situation. After several minutes of repeated counting from one to five, they both shouted, "Nine-one-one. Nine-one-one."

Slowly slipping sideways, chair by chair, I managed to take myself out of the center of the action. By the time the emergency crew arrived, I had nearly made it to the other side of the table. I couldn't see what they were doing to Twyman, but their actions certainly seemed competent. The room, which had produced a varied cacophony of sounds following the initial realization of stunned silence, now was quiet as a tomb again. Janie stood behind me, her strong fingers digging into my shoulder.

Finally the EMTs looked at each other and the attending physicians and shook their heads. "Let's get him to the hospital," one said, although it was evident even to me that the morgue was the obvious destination. None of the professionals would take the responsibility of declaring Twyman deceased, but I heard the woman doctor whisper to the luncheon's chairperson, Elaine Madison, ". . . as a doornail." And down Texas way, doornails are always dead.

Two

The fellowship hall of the Arlington church where the library luncheon took place was ultimately cleared. All the patrons and friends of the library had slowly ebbed out. Of course they bought all the books that Twyman's publisher had sent for the postluncheon author signing. Although these books would never be signed, I guess the purchasers thought they would have some value. "This is Twyman Towerie's first best-seller. I bought it at the luncheon where he died." Things like that amaze me. Sorta like *Elvis Slept Here* signs on the roadside.

Even the catering crew had folded their tables before Janie and I left.

We didn't stay out of shock or idle curiosity but rather so I could collect my shoe from under the table. The area where I had sat . . . next to the deceased . . . was monopolized by official figures following the removal of the body, and I hadn't had a chance to fish around for my left shoe.

"Did you finish with the police? Did they recognize your name?" Janie headed toward my former luncheon chair with me, her arms full of packaged lunches—we didn't get to finish lunch after all—and her Friends of the Library luncheon goodie bag. Her copy of Twyman's best-seller, *For All the Wrong Reasons,* was stuck in her oversized straw purse. We always carry straw bags in the summer in Texas. Its sorta de rigueur, like no velvet in the hot months and no white after Labor Day.

"Yes, I told them all I knew, which was nothing. And no, they don't know me. Not everyone thinks finding dead bodies is a claim to fame, Janie. Now, where is that shoe?" I shuffled over and lifted the white tablecloth.

"Here." Janie dumped her parcels on the table. "Let me find it. You're overbalanced." Her gray-brown-blond head dipped under the table, leaving only a view of an ample Janie backside. "Got it," came her muffled declaration. "And, oh, Honey, here's your goodie bag. She pulled my black patent leather shoe from under the table along with the white plastic bag stamped with the Arlington, Texas, Public Library logo.

She straightened up, holding the bag aloft.

"Honey, would it be cricket if we took Twyman's, too?"

"Twyman's what?"

"His goodie bag. It's down there. I don't want to be indecent, but . . ." Her voice trailed off, her eyes aglow.

I don't know what it is about women, but Janie is no different than the other two hundred women who attended the luncheon or any luncheon where there are goodie bags. There's something really telling about seeing women in Nieman Marcus dresses and Ferragamo shoes grab their freebie sacks filled with commercial giveaways. Why a ten-cent wooden ruler stamped with Eat at A&W is so valuable is beyond me. I don't attend that many functions, but watching them compare and switch contents seems to be a modern-day version of a treasure hunt with the treasure being something they wouldn't have in their house on a dare.

"Janie," I protested.

"Oh, shoot. Who will miss it? Who would

know?'' She dove back under the table, turning her bobbed head floorward again.

Janie fluttered her lashes at me as she stuck Twyman's plastic sack into her own. ''We'll divvy it up back at your house.''

I put on my errant high-heeled sandal and rolled my eyes in response.

Elaine was still in the foyer talking to reporters. I gave her a five-finger wiggle as we edged toward the glass doors, but she wasn't letting me off that lightly.

''Here's one of our guests, Honey Huckleberry. She was sitting next to Mr. Towerie.''

The reporters turned as one, leaving Elaine behind as they swooped down on me. Janie ran her fingers through her hair, mussed from the under-the-table retrieval of shoes and sundries. A woman with a microphone in her hand led a cameraman by a cable like a dog on a leash.

''You were sitting next to Mr. Towerie when he died? Did he have any last words? Did you know he was dead? He's famous, you know.'' She motioned to the cameraman to turn the tape on.

''No, really,'' I protested. ''I don't know anything. We had just sat down a few minutes before he died.''

"Huckleberry? Honey Huckleberry?" This from a man with a notebook. "Didn't we do a story on you in the paper awhile back? Something about a murder?"

"No. Yes. I mean yes, I'm Honey Huckleberry, but I don't know anything about Mr. Towerie's death." I glared at Elaine, who was looking frazzled. I could see that she was weighing the value of the publicity for the library against the notoriety.

With Janie sticking a finger in my back like a gun, I smiled for the cameras, knowing that my five-foot-two redheaded self was being fed into the revolving wheels of news-at-five tape.

Abbie Petunia or some such name went into her spiel: "We have Honey Huckleberry here with us. The famous murder author was also a guest at the ill-fated luncheon for the legendary Twyman Towerie. In fact, Ms. Huckleberry was sitting next to the writer when he died. Tell me, Ms. Huckleberry. Did Mr. Towerie have any premonition of his death? What were his last words?" Then Ms. Gardenia—I finally read the ID tag right—thrust the fuzzy end of the microphone at me.

I continued to smile, wondering if I should correct her about my being an author, until Janie jabbed me again. "Yes, I was sitting next to Mr. Towerie."

Gardenia turned the mike toward herself again as if she was going to take a bite of it. "And what was the conversation?"

It was my turn to snack at the black fuzzy again. Like some other professions, I guess it's all in the wrist, this turning the microphone back and forth. I was fascinated. I leaned forward for my nibble. No wonder they called them *sound bites.* "He was very pleasant. We really only exchanged a few words about the luncheon. How we hoped it would raise money for the Arlington Library." I smiled and resisted wiping my lips.

Her bite.

"Was he in distress? Did you know he was going to die? Did *he?*" She persisted with the gore theme.

I continued to lie.

"It was so sudden. I'm sure he never knew what hit him." Now *that* was probably the truth.

Disappointed and giving me a glare, Ms. Abbie Rose Gardenia Petunia devoured the microphone again with her closing words. I didn't hear them. Janie and I were out the door.

"Hmmm . . . Honey, you lied to her." I don't know when Janie began knowing me so well.

"Hmmm . . ." I murmured back. "You're right."

"Give," was the one-word order.

I don't know why I always lie to police and wind

up telling Janie the truth. "What he said was . . ." I whispered into her ear as we crossed the street to the parking lot into the hot, humid day. " 'Can you tell me how one goes about finding out if someone is trying to kill them?' "

"I knew it. I knew it. I just smelled it all along. It *was* murder, wasn't it, Honey?"

Three

I live on the south side of Fort Worth. I know I ought to move, but what can I say? The three-storied asbestos-siding house is my legacy, my security, and my burden. I reckon I should put bars on the windows, but that would be like closing the barn door after the cows are gone. If there were any kids left in the neighborhood, my house would be the one they would point to as "the murder house" when they hurried by. Instead of youngsters passing, I had scores of cars headed toward their drivers' appointed hours at the various clinics and doctors' offices that had encrypted the neighborhood. My house is the last holdout against tongue depressors and eye patches.

It's busy during the day around my place, but at night, it's blessedly quiet. Just me and the house and the money. How many of the day people would believe I had four million dollars in cash hidden in the upright piano in the dining room? It was the people of the night I worried about.

Well, Janie would believe.

If I told her.

Which I hadn't.

One of the few secrets I had kept from her.

The only person who knew of the cash cache was my accountant and financial adviser Steven Bondesky, and he wasn't very happy with me.

Bondesky called me daily to see if I had done anything about my *big* problem. That was his way of encoding a message. Like my phones are wiretapped or something. Oh, on second thought, *his* might be.

After we reached home from the library luncheon, Janie fussed around in the kitchen, putting the catered lunch onto my Desert Rose dishes, pretending that we had cooked the baked chicken and smashed the mashed potatoes. A pass through my new microwave and linen napkins contributed to the illusion, but as we sat down to eat, we both knew that it was a sham meal. A dead man's last meal.

Oh, well, we ate it anyway.

As I toyed with the green beans, I thought of saying out loud, "Janie, I've been meaning to tell you. Two months ago, when we had all that murder stuff going on, I found the money my father left me. It was in the walls of the house, and now I've crammed it into the piano behind you. What do you think I should do with it?"

"Four," said Janie.

She knew?

"Well, maybe over four," I responded.

Janie laughed. "Yes, if you can count the first one twice."

"What?"

"He married the first wife twice."

"Janie, what are you talking about?"

She looked up from a forkful of potatoes. "Why, Twyman. He had four wives, but was married five times. Wonder which one killed him?"

"Silly, you're always looking for the murderer. Twyman wasn't murdered. He died of a coronary or something. Big men like that have heart attacks at the snap of a finger." And I demonstrated, snapping.

Janie was profound. "Honey, there is more murder in the world than we know. And you said your-self that he told you someone was trying to kill him.''

''No, I said he asked if I knew what to do if you thought someone was trying to kill you. There's a difference, Janie. It's like polite talk.''

She snorted. ''Ha! I'm the only one I know who thinks murder is part of polite talk. And politeness and Towerie don't belong together in the same sentence.'' She scraped up the last of her mashed potatoes and beans, stuffing it in her mouth with a *so there* attitude. ''Now,'' she said, as she lifted her iced tea glass, swirling the melting ice in the last of the drink, ''tell me every single word he said.''

As I told her about my surprise at being seated beside the guest of honor and the subsequent remarks we had exchanged, Janie kept nodding her head for me to go on as she cleared the table, carrying the empty plates to the kitchen and returning with the lemon pie.

''He laughed at you?''

''Yes. When I asked him where he lived.''

''Just like that? You asked him where he lived, and he laughed? Hmmm,'' she muttered, rolling the thought over in her head like it was a clue.

''Not exactly.'' I sighed.

I was born to and reared by two very elderly people. Until they died ten years ago when I was eighteen, I spent the majority of my time with them. They loved and cherished me as well as giving me some very quaint and antiquated manners. I have spent my adult life trying to reconcile that upbringing against the sometimes harsh realities of a late-twentieth-century world.

Flustered at being seated by one of the world's greatest authors, I had stammered, "And where do you make your home, Mr. Towerie?" Thereby providing the man with his last laugh on earth.

"*Where do I make my home?*" He had sputtered into his coffee cup. "Girl, that phrase went out in the twenties. Where did you come up with that one? And here I thought you were some big, hotshot detective." And he repeated his favorite new phrase. "Where do you *make* your home?"

I wanted to tell him that calling a woman *girl* was also gone from the modern PC vocabulary, but instead, I asked in surprise, "Detective? Me? Where did you get that idea?"

"From the papers. It was on the news wire everywhere about how you found two dead bodies and solved an international mystery. Any of that true?" Skeptical was the least of the looks Twyman imparted to me over raised eyebrows.

"Oh, that. Surely you know that newspapers always get it wrong. It is true that two men died in my house. Well," I corrected, "one in the parking lot. And there was an international scandal, yes. It was all about alternative fuel formulas and . . ." I faltered.

And cut to the chase.

"It just all *happened* to me, Mr. Towerie. I didn't have anything to do with originating the mystery. Other people in other places and other times started the chain of events."

"Oh." He had looked disappointed out of proportion to the discussion. "And here I was going to ask for your help."

"*My* help? With what?"

I finally came to the part Janie wanted repeated.

Twyman shrugged as he answered, "I was going to ask you how one goes about finding out if someone is trying to kill them." His disappointment had quickly changed to a grin as he took the lemon pie that was offered by the server as she also set his baked chicken plate in front of him. He greedily reached forward with his fork and—well, Janie knew the rest of that story.

With my background, I have trouble saying *wow*, but the same parents obviously did not rear Janie and me.

"Wow," she said. "What on earth do you think he meant?"

"I think it meant he was researching some new work and wanted an insight into the detective's viewpoint. Which he mistakenly thought I was."

"Could be," she replied. "Or could be it was a genuine plea for assistance."

I finished cleaning off the table.

"That man had more money than God," I said. "He could have hired the best detective minds in the country. It was just an idle question, Janie. Had nothing really to do with me."

As I placed the dirty dishes into my new dishwasher—I *had* spent a wee bit of the piano money—the phone rang.

Janie caught it for me, talked a few minutes, and came into the kitchen with a satisfied smile on her face. "So much for coincidence," she said.

Continuing, she answered my unasked question. "That was Elaine from Arlington on the phone. She's still shook up about Twyman's death. Wanted to know if *you* were all right. Seemed to think you knew Twyman."

"Everyone knew Twyman Towerie. He wrote three of the greatest books in the world," I said.

"No, she meant *really* knew him." She smiled

smugly. "Seems the great man agreed to come to the Friends of the Arlington Public Library luncheon only when she agreed to invite *you* and have *you* sit beside him."

"Good lord," I said.

Four

I couldn't believe I diverted Janie from Twyman talk by actually saying "Wow." (I'm practicing my wows.) "Let's see what's in our goodie bags."

She grinned as she remembered the unsorted treasure. "You clear the table, and I'll spread it all out. One side for you and one for me. We'll add Twyman's lot later."

I chose the left side of the table and received:

1 white coffee cup from First Bank of Arlington
1 red notepad with RX from Eckerd Drugs

1 flat twelve-inch wooden ruler from Mrs. Baird's
Bakery

3 after-dinner mints (no logo)

6 shrink-wrapped paper plates from Jason's Deli

1 30%-off coupon from Shelton's Beauty Salon

1 navy blue sun visor from the *Star-Telegram*

1 fall class catalog from the University of Texas at
Arlington

1 paper bookmark from Barnes & Noble

1 coupon good for 50% off a frozen coffee from
Borders Books

Janie got:

1 white coffee cup from First Bank of Arlington

1 red notepad with RX from Eckerd Drugs

1 flat 12-inch wooden ruler from Mrs. Baird's
Bakery

3 after-dinner mints (no logo)

6 shrink-wrapped paper plates from Jason's Deli

1 30%-off coupon from Shelton's Beauty Salon

1 navy blue sun visor from the *Star-Telegram*

1 fall class catalog from the University of Texas at
Arlington

1 paper bookmark from Barnes & Noble

1 coupon good for 50% off of a frozen coffee from
   Borders Books

Janie smiled. "What a haul."

"Well, yes," I replied weakly.

"Now to divide Twyman's bag. Honey, do you mind if I take the coffee cup? I always keep free coffee for customers at Pages, and I just hate paper cups."

"Be my guest."

"And what do you want in exchange?" she asked seriously.

"Oh, well, the after-dinner mints, I think. And—" I reached into the plastic bag, "—this." I held up a small white box.

"What's that? We didn't get a *box.* How come Twyman got a box? Who's it from? What's in it?"

"I don't know. Honest. I just reached in and came up with it. You can have it."

"Oh, no, you chose it. It's yours. But what is it?"

Janie could hardly wait for me to open the small package. It reminded me of Christmas or birthdays where you were almost beside yourself over a wrapped box until you opened it. Then you said, "Oh, a robe. Just what I wanted." And turned your enthusiasm to the next mystery package.

"It's from Haltom's," I said, reading the gold letters embossed on the box.

"*We* didn't get anything from Haltom's," Janie said. "Reckon it was special because it was for the guest of honor's bag?" Just to make sure we hadn't missed a surprise box in our bags, she ran a hand over both the empty sacks. "Wonder if he got anything else special?" She overturned Twyman's bag onto the table. "Nope, just the regular stuff left here. Come on, Honey, open it, for Pete's sake."

"Do you think we should?"

Janie gave me a bear's-in-the-woods look, which I took for a yes.

"Hmmm."

"Let me see," she clamored.

"It's a ring." I held it up.

"A diamond ring," Janie gasped.

"Oh, I'm sure it's not. Real, that is. A giveaway gimmick from Haltom's. How clever of them to put it in the bag of the only person in the room who could probably afford a ring this size." I laughed.

Janie took the ring from me and turned it around her hand. "No, Honey, it's a real one." And she pointed to the hallmark inside. "Eighteen-karat gold."

"Couldn't possibly be," I replied just as if I knew what a real diamond looked like. "It's not even

diamond-shiny. It's sorta pink." I repeated firmly,
"It's a gimmick, Janie."

"Yes, I guess you are right. We'd be too lucky
to have a real diamond fall into our hands."

She glanced at her watch. "Oops, gotta run. I told
the woman minding the store I'd be back before
school was out so she could pick up her kids."

I checked the time on my watch. "Well, you're
not going to make it. It will be way after three by
the time you make it home." The town of West,
Texas, was a little over an hour from Fort Worth.

"I gave her a key to Pages so she'll just have
locked up and gone on, but I do need to get back.
I want to be home for the early news. To see what
they say about Twyman's murder."

I grinned. Janie, enamoured with her mystery
books, would make a mystery out of an anthill. We
had been business acquaintances for a few years:
Pages was one of the small-town bookstores where
I stopped on my route to do inventory and promote
the list I carried for several small presses. It was
only the recent past circumstances that made the two
of us become closer than just a professional relationship. Having faced a murderer in our midst had
certainly altered both our lives.

The faux diamond was forgotten on the dining
room table as Janie bustled about, gathering up her

purse and goodie-bag loot. For a small, rotund woman, she certainly stirred a stream of energy in her path. But I remembered that when she faded, she went downhill fast. "Drive carefully," I admonished. I hated it, but I always seemed to have to say all the cautionary warnings my mother had extolled to me. It was like a mantra. If I didn't say them, something bad was sure to happen.

Janie was always tickled when I went into my motherly mode. "Yes'm," she said and blew me a kiss as she hastened down the walk to her car.

I watched her affectionately as she drove off.

Some people might call her naive. But since I had a patent on the appellation, I genuinely delighted in her innocent enthusiasm about everything that crossed her path. It was like seeing the world through new eyes to be around Janie for very long. Take, for instance, her obstinacy in declaring Twyman a murder victim. All I had seen was an overweight, middle-aged man who had succumbed to the stress and excesses of his successful writing career. Janie had seen a murder plot.

The author of only three books in his lifetime, Twyman had been a true minimalist. Every word in his books counted and was inestimable. His fame was truly deserved and his talent unquestionable. That his manners left something to be desired could be excused. Geniuses were seldom appreciated in their reality, but it didn't matter. Just their creative outpourings were enough.

Which was good for the deceased, because in real life he had been a real . . . I searched for a word that wouldn't offend the wisps of my mother's ghostly ears. I came up with *horse's putootie* Okay, a little old-fashioned. I smiled. Twyman would have loved that one. It would have killed him.

Five

Once or twice a month, I meet with my personal financial planner and accountant to go over my figures. This was a dutiful routine I had assumed since my parents had died—within a day of each other—when I was eighteen. Steven Bondesky had not presumed to undertake a parental role, and our relationship was one of love and hate and give and take that had altered considerably when I had accused him wrongly of murder earlier in the year.

He had spent some time in the Tarrant County Jail at my behest and, although he wasn't guilty of the homicide of my friend Steven Miller or his friend Jimmy, he had been investigated for other odd aspects of his business. He had forgiven me for the false accusation but still glowered over the intrusion into his professional life.

Tired as I was from the morning and early afternoon excitement, I was too aroused to take a nap or curl up with a new book.

So, since I was wired for action anyway, I headed off to visit the bear in his den.

There had been some changes in the west side building that Bondesky called his office and, for all I knew, his home. Fresh black asphalt poured out onto the street, giving the appearance of a parking lot. Since there were some gray dusty tracks of car wheels on it, I decided it was ready to receive my Plymouth Voyager and parked in the three-car-wide space.

On the new aluminum screen door was a five-inch brass plate announcing Bondesky Financial Services, and a concrete urn by the entrance sprouted freshly planted purple petunias. "Bondesky," I thought, "I hardly know ye."

The front office was just as much a surprise. There was an actual desk with a live secretarial-type woman sitting there. You coulda knocked me over with a feather. The usual riffraff of upchucked derelicts was absent and Muzak was playing over a

recently installed speaker bolted high on the wall.
There was even a picture on the wall: a three-by-
five-foot print of Ophelia down by the riverside.

"How may I help you?" asked the perfectly
coiffed, silver-haired woman at the desk.

"Uh, I'm here to see Bondesky," I replied.

"May I tell him who is calling? And the purpose
of your visit?"

"Uh, Honey Huckleberry. And . . . er . . . on business."

She rose, showing off shapely legs and a tiny
waist in her navy blue cotton suit.

"One moment, Miss Huckleberry. I'll see if Mr.
Bondesky is available." She picked up her memo
pad and pen and headed toward the closed office
door behind her desk.

I pinched myself to make sure I was in the right
place. Where was the dirty linoleum? The grungy
coffeepot with the hangers-on? The cops who always stopped by for free donuts and a pee break?
For God's sake, there were magazines on the table
next to upholstered chairs. I crossed the freshly laid
blue carpet and checked them out. *U.S. News and
World Report*? *Money Magazine*? And they were
current issues.

"Ahem, Miss Huckleberry? Mr. Bondesky asked
that you wait for a few minutes. Is that convenient

for you?'' Miss Perfect Secretary quietly closed the
inner door and slipped back into her desk slot.

"Wait? Well, yes, I guess I could *wait*."

"Wonderful," she said. "May I get you some
coffee?"

"No, I'm fine, thanks."

We smiled at one another and listened to Tchai-
kovsky's Symphony No. 6, "Pathetique," over the
speaker. At least that's what the erudite announcer's
voice *said* we were going to be enjoying.

"My favorite," I said.

"You, too?" she responded. In surprise.

"I don't know your name," I told her as the
promised music pleasured our ears.

"Evelyn Potter. My nameplate"—and she gestured to the waiting spot on her desk—"hasn't arrived yet."

"Ah."

There was a subtle buzz from somewhere on her
desk.

"You may go in now, Miss Huckleberry. Are you
sure I can't get you some coffee? A soft drink?
Tea?"

"No, thank you. And it's been a pleasure, Ms.
Potter."

The final straw in this made-for-TV pageant was
that Bondesky was wearing a tie, albeit a poorly tied

one; blue with a huge rainbow trout leaping for the ultimate lure, which rested somewhere in the loosened collar of his shirt.

"Where's your eyeshade?" I asked.

"I got a new light. Don't need it."

I looked up. "Right. Where's the card table?"

"I got this office module. Computer fits it better."

"Right."

He looked defensive. I looked belligerent. I'm not into changes much.

I was used to going into a tough-girl act when I was with Bondesky. He was the one who had taught me the value of sarcasm: like Epsom salts, it toughened my soul. This patina of legitimacy was doing me in. It was like when I was a little girl and I *cleaned* up my playroom by putting my mother's old evening gowns over the mess. The room sparkled with net and glitter, but the mess was still underneath. She had praised me anyhow.

"Looks great," I told Bondesky. I always remember my mother's lessons.

We coulda gone on pretending, but underneath it all, Bondesky and I shared the same weird sense of humor. We did a chicken stare-down for a few seconds and then both burst into laughter.

The laughter was healing. It wiped away all the

guilt I felt and all the resentment he harbored.

Bondesky bobbed his head and motioned me closer.

"Ain't this something?"

"Absolutely. Why did you do it?"

"Well, my lawyer told me if my joint had looked more respectable, I wouldn't have had to stay in jail so long. They thought I was doing something illegal here."

"No. Imagine that."

"Yep. Hard to believe. Me. Doing something illegal. When everyone knows I was just keeping overhead down to better serve my clients."

"Bondesky?"

"Yes?"

"Why are we whispering?"

"Its *her.*"

"That Ms. Patton? I mean Potter. She just acts like Patton."

"Yes, she's so . . . so . . . I don't know the word."

"Professional?"

"Yeah, that, too."

I straightened from my stoop over the desk. "Bondesky, what happened to the boys?"

"Aw, Huckleberry, I wouldn't forget my boys." Bondesky reverted to normal tones, too. *Let her listen* seemed to be an unspoken motto we assumed.

"I built them a prefab place out back. You ought to see it. Got me a pool table and real coffee machine. The guys love it. They call it Jimmy's Place."

We smiled in remembrance of the man who had died to protect me; a derelict Bondesky had nursed since the mentally injured man had returned from Vietnam. "He would have liked that," I said.

The momentary mist that clouded the old man's eyes lifted as he cleared his froggy throat and asked, "So, what can I do for you?"

"I want to buy a computer."

Bondesky got excited. Now that he didn't wear the old green eyeshade, I could actually see emotions in his pale blue eyes. "Now you're talking." He reached across the desk to shake my hand. "Welcome to the twentieth century, Huckleberry."

As old as he was, Bondesky had been on the cutting edge of the computer revolution, using it for business long before others. The equipment had changed shape and function over the years, but it seemed to me that he had always had some kind of monitor glowing in the background. Even when I used to come with my father to visit.

He took out a pen. "Whadda you want?"

"How should I know?"

"Well, what do you want it to do for you?"

"Keep my schedule? Client list? Addresses?"

"Okay. What else?"

"I don't know. What else is there? I've never had one before, remember."

"Expenses would be good," said the accountant in him.

"Yes, starting with all that, what do I need?" ·

He churched his pudgy fingers together, rubbing the steeple part over his shiny nose, thinking.

"Might as well start with the best. I'll special order a Dell for you from Austin. Get customized programs. You'll have to get a second phone line. And we'll get you a laptop from Mike Dell, too. For the road." He pressed a button on his phone. She showed up, memo pad in hand.

"Miz Patton. I have a job for you." Bondesky sounded happy to have found some work for her. He rattled off names and numbers to her that she almost wrote down before he said them. She was really fast.

"And we send the bill to Miss Huckleberry? How will she be paying?"

"Any way she wants to," he said. "But probably with cash?" He raised a bushy eyebrow in my direction.

"Probably." I smiled.

Maybe Bondesky would make it in the real world. He dismissed Ms. Secretary and leaned forward. I inched toward the desk. I sensed another whisper session.

"What?"

"You've got to do something about the money."

"It's safe."

"No. It's not."

"Lightning does not strike twice. No one knows about the money. Except you. And Steven Hyatt."

"I worry about that part. But I also worry about you not putting it into investments. Four million dollars won't last forever, Huckleberry. Especially not the way you're spending it."

"What do you mean? So, I bought a dishwasher. A few things for the house. I haven't gone to Hawaii yet," I protested.

"Nah, I mean like the jewelry."

"Hey, I buy my earrings at Claire's."

Bondesky pointed toward my hand. "You didn't buy that at no boutique. Or maybe it's a gift? From one of your hordes of boyfriends? Let me guess. I know it ain't Steven Hyatt. So . . . the guy from Italy or the one from the valley? The one with the dog."

I looked down in surprise. When I left the house, I had picked up the ring from Twyman's goodie bag, intending to put it in the catchall drawer of the dining room breakfront, but instead, I had slipped it on my finger for transportation purposes as I collected my purse and my keys. Then I had forgotten to leave it in the drawer. I had noticed it on my drive over, the sun reflecting colorful sparkly rainbows onto the interior of the van. During my visit with Bondesky, unused to wearing a ring, I had twisted it around my finger.

"Oh, the ring," I exclaimed. "It's not real. I found it. Sorta. Which reminds me. I'm going to be on the six o'clock news. But don't worry. It wasn't murder, no matter what Janie thinks. He was just a glutton. And a real horse's patootie." I blushed. Lord, my language was deteriorating.

"I don't know what you're talking about, Huckleberry. Who died this time?" He stood up and reached across the desk to catch my hand. His short, rough fingers turned the ring right side up on my finger. "I do know this, though. This here ring is real."

Six

"This has been a strange day," I muttered to myself as I inched through the Taco Bell drive-through on my way home. I gave my taco salad order and tapped my fingers on the wheel. The only ring I had on my hand flashed in the glare of a late-afternoon sun and the interior of the car lit up like the Rose-land Ballroom. If what Bondesky had said was true, I was wearing several hundred thousands of dollars on my ring finger.

I had settled a hip on Bondesky's new desk and told him about my very strange day. Beginning with the luncheon with Twyman, I simply and factually told about the author's death at my elbow, the goodie bags, and the ring. Oh, and the television interview.

He didn't blink a beady eye. Took a new death in my life as normal, but did surprise me when he said he knew Twyman. Had *known* Twyman. "He was a skinny twerp back then. Eager like a puppy dog. Strange look in his eyes. Never did know what Clover saw in him. Why she married him."

I thought of the corpulent man who had died today. It was hard to imagine Twyman as ever young or skinny. "Who's Clover?"

"His first wife. Clover Medlock. Ask me, and I'll say that he took her for a ride. Told her so at the time. I'd have married her myself, but he was smarter. Better looking. I wasn't as successful or as distinguished looking then like I am now."

I let that one go.

"I seem to remember from the bios. He started out here, right?"

"Yeah, was a half-baked reporter from Weatherford. Did a big story on Clover and got on her good side. Then romanced her. He was a writer. Knew those romance words." Bondesky had grimaced. Romance to him was the glow of his computer monitor.

"What was the story about?"

"You ain't heard of Clover Medlock? She's the one who developed a new breed of cattle. Some kind of Brangus or somesuch. All by herself. Well, sir, it was a big story all right. Little pretty lady ranching and driving her tractor all over the place. Down near Granbury. Know the area?"

"Yes, I have a client there. Small bookstore I visit. Is she still alive then?"

He had smiled an old rogue smile. "Oh, yes. Oh, yes."

Before I ate the taco salad with the extra sour cream, I remembered to call Silas. He was the only other one I worried about hearing my name or seeing me on the news associated with another deceased body.

I noticed Bondesky had left Silas Sampson off the boyfriend list, and it was an accurate call. Silas was a policeman, detective actually, and while we had flirted with the idea of what Bondesky called romancing, we had never progressed beyond the eyelash-fluttering stage.

Silas wasn't in, but I left a message on his voice mail. "Silas, Honey. Don't worry. It was natural causes." And I had added, "I'm sure."

So with a glass of iced tea and my cardboard box plate from Taco Bell, I settled in front of the television in the living room. This was new to me, eating in the living room. But it was getting close to 5:30 and I thought the death of someone of Twyman's stature would probably make the national news.

I was right. Not only did they mention his death, but they also showed videos of him with all four of his ex-wives. Wow. They were all celebrities, too, although I only recognized the movie star, Babe.

It was on the local 6 o'clock news that I was mentioned. Oh, there had been a white-faced glimpse of me on the national news, but no one knew me, so who would notice?

Steven Hyatt, of course.

Since I now have caller ID, I could see it was him calling. I could answer or I could watch the local news. Steven Hyatt was my best friend ever, so I picked up the insistently ringing phone and said, "Georgie Porgie, pudding and pie. I'll call you right back." And hung up.

Abby Gardenia was almost breathless with her excitement on getting to report Twyman's death. Since it happened in Fort Worth, there was a sure bet the report was getting a national feed and would be rebroadcast from coast to coast. It was interesting watching her audition her stuff. Until she came to me.

You're supposed to look ten pounds heavier on

television, so I reckon I am really skinny. I looked like an orange-headed, frizzy wraith next to Ms. Gardenia's full-flown Italian coloring. Or was it makeup? I moved closer to the big screen to check.

"Yes, I was sitting next to Mr. Towerie."

"And what was the conversation?"

"He was very pleasant. We really only exchanged a few words about the luncheon. How we hoped it would raise money for the Arlington Library."

"Was he in distress? Did you know he was going to die? Did he?"

"It was so sudden. I'm sure he never knew what hit him."

And so on.

At the end of my interview, I sighed. That wasn't so bad. No mention of Steven Miller or Jimmy the Geek. Just the usual *I was there when he fell over dead* stuff. I eased back into my chair to watch the roundup on the story. A police official came on and said how the woman doctor had accompanied the body to the hospital and pronounced Twyman dead of natural causes. No foul play suspected.

So it had been totally unnecessary for me to call Silas Sampson to inform him of the death. Especially since Silas had been the police official who spoke so professionally about the author's death, his blond good looks vying for space on my television screen with Ms. Gardenia's dark, sultry shape. They made a good-looking couple. Gardenia must have thought so, too. There were ten Arlington cops standing around, but it was Silas, the Fort Worth police detective, she had chosen to interview.

Seven

Steven Hyatt and I had been best friends since high school. He was a nice kid who had impressed my father so they had made a deal whereby Steven profited from driving me home every day from school and my father could stay with my ailing mother. We wound up becoming chums, insulating ourselves from others as we studied and made up games in the third floor of my south side house. Always under the watchful eyes of my father who read his newspaper while Steven and I obliviously reworked the world.

One of our games had been the "saving" of un-

known poets who seemed to us like spirits who had
offered up their immortal words only to have their
names forgotten, though their work lived on through
countless anthologies. As it was our *duty* to save
these poor lost souls, we had memorized their lines
and used them as code words to communicate.

In the sometimes cruel, good old school days, the
game provided us with a belonging that was denied
by our social status. Steven was an orphaned intellectual who lived with a maiden aunt, and I was the
skinny misfit who had the very elderly parents. Neither one of us was considered *cool,* except by each
other.

Mother Goose was not on our list of unknowns,
but when I called Steven back in New York following the news, "Georgie Porgie" was the only poem
that seemed appropriate for the situation.

"Georgie Porgie, pudding and pie . . ." I said into
the telephone.

"Kissed the girls and made them cry," Steven
Hyatt responded. "But when the boys came out to
play, Georgie Porgie ran away."

"Well, not this one, Steven. He just died."

"So I saw on NBC. Want to tell me about it?"

So I told Steven Hyatt about my very strange day.

As an independent producer and director of a few
noteworthy films, Steven relished the bizarre and

unexpected. I was sure he was curling his toes and running his big bony hands through his frazzled hair as he listened to my pitiful tale of a day gone wrong. At the end, he sighed, but I couldn't tell if it was from rapture or exasperation.

He said unexpectedly, "Honey, maybe it's time for you to settle down and have babies."

"Accck, Steven!"

"No, wait; I mean it. Look, your life has been smooth and safe until this summer when you found murdered men at your house and money in your walls. Thank you for sharing, by the way. The new project is going well. But, well, here you are."

"Not for long. I'm hanging up."

"No, wait. I'm saying this wrong. What I mean is, your life is changing, and if you don't get a handle on it soon, it will be just one catastrophic event after another. Aimless drifting. You need a rock, a base. A husband and a real house and . . . yes, babies."

"Excuse me? I'm the one who has an address, not a hotel room. I'm the one with the regular job. I'm the one who lives by a schedule. You're the one who needs an anchor. Preferably around your neck this minute."

He sighed that long-suffering sigh again. "Honey, I worry about you."

"Steven, you are not my father. You're not even my brother. I don't know what you are, except the last person in the world to be telling me I need a normal life. So what if I sit down by a dead man at lunch? I ate *my* vegetables first."

I hung up on him.

The very idea.

The indignation I felt toward Steven Hyatt spilled over to my conversation with Silas, who was the next immediate caller. Without preamble, recognizing the source from the caller wizard attached to my phone, I answered with, "Go marry that daffodil flower woman and raise daisies."

When he called back, I apologized.

One more call from Janie, and I went to bed. I dearly hate telephones.

I was totally and utterly exhausted. For the first time in my life, I didn't brush my teeth or wash my face.

After such a day, I should have slept the sleep of the dead, but I tussled with my nest of pillows, wishing Steven Hyatt had been acting more like himself. If he had been doing so, I could have told him about the very real fear I had seen in Twyman Towerie's eyes when he had asked me, "Can you tell me how one goes about finding out if someone is trying to kill them?"

Eight

It was almost noon when I entered Haltom's. I'd had two cups of French roasted coffee and a jelly-laden croissant from La Madeleine's next door before I could gather the nerve to visit the jewelers.

I won't say I was intimidated, but I will admit I'm more of a Joe Daiches's type of diamond shopper. Or would have been if I had ever shopped for one. Lower Main Street would have suited me better than the exclusive west side store I entered. I felt like a criminal casing the joint, sentiments shared by the honey blond salesperson whose silk blouse whispered warnings as she approached me.

"Good morning. May I help you?"

It was the old Neiman-Marcus *be nice to the customer even if she is wearing a bathrobe 'cause she may have millions tucked in her pockets* approach. Which, theoretically, I did. Although I was dressed in shorts and a blue 1996 Olympic T-shirt.

"Just looking."

"A gift perhaps? Or something personal?"

I had decided over the croissant that I would act like a customer. Hey, it was time I spent a little on a bauble. I could afford it. "A ring?"

"Engagement? Wedding? Evening?"

For a minute I thought she was asking me if I was getting married that night, then realized she was asking the type of ring I wanted.

I held up my finger. "Which is this?"

She held my hand still in her cool, tapered fingers for a long minute. "Maybe you would like to see our manager?" And she smiled and disappeared beyond the counter.

I stood, waiting amid the heavy air emitted by the equally heavy silver trays and tea sets. Soft music played in the air. My new friend "Pathetique." I would like to say I recognized the tune, but knew of its arrival from the same dulcet-toned voice I had heard at Bondesky's. I wandered around, trying to make the music my own and reached down to smell a fantastic arrangement of giant magnolias. Amazing what they can do with silk these days.

"Excuse me. May I help you?"

I straightened, rubbing imaginary magnolia pollen from my nose, to find an older version of the first helper. I held out my hand again. "Yes, I just wanted to know what this ring is worth."

She looked at it for a long time, exchanged a look with the original salesperson, and asked, "May I have it, please?"

I jerked my hand back. No way.

She smiled. Sorta. Identified herself as Winona Octavia, the manager of Haltom's Camp Bowie store. "I'd like our jeweler to look at the ring, Mrs. Towerie."

"Mrs. Towerie," I repeated.

"Yes," she replied pleasantly. "I would like for our Mr. Bagget to see the ring to confirm its identification. As you must know, we are the ones who sold the ring to your ex-husband." Winona stopped to sigh. "I am so sorry about his shocking death. He was so excited about giving the ring to you."

I didn't say a word.

Winona took me by the hand and led me to a back counter where a pleasant-faced gentleman stood with a loupe in his eye. She didn't ask me for the ring again but simply placed my whole hand on a black velvet square on the counter. The man swooped forward to examine the ring. I felt like I was having my teeth X-rayed at the dentist and should stop the examination for a lead apron. Instead, I smiled at Winona, who smiled at me. "Pathetique" played on.

Then the man smiled and nodded to Winona, who smiled at *him* and then turned to bestow another on me. "Yes, of course, it's the very same ring," she declared. "I knew it, but I wanted you to be reassured. Do you want to see the original receipt?"

I smiled yes.

Winona continued to chat in such a pleasant manner as she searched a back counter that I wondered if she doubled as a Muzak disc jockey on the side. "Again, we were so shocked to hear about Mr. Towerie's death. Such a delightful man. And so thrilled to have found the perfect ring for you. I imagine you're having it appraised for the estate? You don't have to do that, you know. As a gift, the ring belongs to you now. But I'm sure you want it for your insurance company. Ah, here it is." And she returned with a yellow sheet of paper. "I can make a copy for you if you like."

I liked.

I breathed deep into the sultry Texas sunshine when I shut the jewelry store door behind me. The eleven o'clock humid air jarred me awake from the sleepwalker me who had actually impersonated another and walked away with falsified papers. I pursed my lips to break the permanent smile pasted there since Winona had first called me Mrs. Towerie and I hadn't done one thing to clarify the situation.

"It's not a falsified piece of paper. Just falsely acquired," Janie cheerfully reassured me when I called her from the cell phone in my van. "Don't worry about it. Now, tell me. What does it say? How much is that ring worth?"

"Well, for starters, you and Bondesky were right. It's the real thing, all right. Three hundred thousand dollars' worth of real thing. This thing is an oval cut champagne diamond."

"Of course, that's where it gets its pinkish color. I should have known," she interrupted. "Oh, Honey, I am so proud of you. Your very first ever undercover work."

"I didn't intend to go undercover," I protested. "I meant to be above the covers. I meant to be honest, but I just didn't say I wasn't who she thought I was. Mrs. Towerie, I mean."

"Yes, yes. Undercover."

"What do I do now?"

"You know what I would do. Just enjoy the ring.

But, knowing you, I'd say you would be trying to give the ring back, right?''

''Right,'' I agreed.

''She called Twyman your ex? That means the ring was intended for one of his ex-wives. Dear me, where to start?''

''I know,'' I said slowly.

''You know one of his ex-wives?''

''No, but I know someone who does.''

Nine

I am an avid map-reader and Triple A knows me well.

Every time I get a new bookstore assignment from company headquarters, I rush to AΛA and have them carefully show me the best route, which I immediately place in my big red plastic notebook titled: How to get there. If I don't do the above, I wind up wandering country roads, gazing up at the sun trying to remember if the sun sets in the east or the west. I've come a long way in remembering it's not north or south.

I've come to the conclusion that directions are a guy thing.

Since I had to get back on the road on Monday, I resorted to asking Bondesky the way to Clover Medlock's farm when I called him to ask for an introduction to the lady rancher. Knowing my proclivity for getting it wrong, I set out early Friday morning, and sure enough, the sun was high overhead by the time I navigated the back roads. Which did me no good at all. High sun just means noon to me.

Yep, there was the silver bridge.

Yep, there was the dead end road.

It was great seeing them, an affirmation of the crisscrossed roads I had maneuvered, but the question remained: where was Clover's ranch?

Surely that rusty-red collection of pipes and gates that leaned against each other down the left side of the road was not part of it? Oops, make that the right side of the road. East and west are not the only directions with which I have problems.

Since there was a large black flatbed truck parked near the side of the road, I opted for at least asking directions. Again.

When I got out of the van, I was struck once more by the unrelenting heat of a Texas summer. The only thing worse than Fort Worth in the summer is Hous-

ton in the summer, which didn't make me smile.
Houston was my Monday's destination.

Thinking ahead, I had worn my heavy tennis
shoes on the trip, which really wasn't all that far
from Fort Worth. Across the flat land weighted
down by a cloudless blue sky, I could still see the
outlines of the city off to the west. East?

Even with wearing denim shorts and a light blue
denim sleeveless shirt, I was soaked by the time I
reached the cowhand distributing some kind of food
from a shoulder hanging bag to the assorted livestock gathered around him. I wiped my hand across
my brow and up into the curly mass of hair that was
sweat-soaked and springy to my touch. "Pardon me,
but I need some directions."

"You're late."

"Pardon me?"

"If you're a Honey Huckleberry, you're late."

"Yes, I am, and I am so sorry." With my apol-
ogy, the tall cowhand turned around to reveal a
woman of conflicting features. Maybe it was because Bondesky had pulled an old black and white
photo out of his desk, showing me the young Clover
Medlock, but as I stared at the lined, weathered
woman before me, I found it hard to recognize the
same features I had seen in the photograph.

"Ms. Medlock?"

"That's my name. And yours is Honey. Together we make quite a breakfast treat, huh?"

I laughed in spite of myself. I hadn't put the two names together. Clover honey with huckleberry jam.

The lines in Clover Medlock's face could have been intimidating or cynical, but when she crinkled them into a hoarse laugh, they lent a pleasant frame to her wide-set hazel eyes. "Steven says you're good people."

"Steven? Oh, you mean Bondesky? Thank you. It was kind of him to call you for me. And for you to see me."

"So, what's so urgent, Honey Huckleberry?" Her honest eyes stared into mine from beneath her crisp felt Stetson. It was either new or Clover wasn't feeling the heat as I was. My SOS pad of frizzy wet hair would have taken the style out of the hat as soon as I stepped out of the van.

"I'm sure Bondesky told you. It's about Twyman Towerie."

With that, the woman closed her eyes. Not her lids, just the inside-looking-out eyes. Like a screen door protecting a porch. She swerved and continued to throw pellets out to the herd that had continued to gather around us. Her words belied her self-protection as she resumed talking. "Yes, this is a

Twyman morning, all right. He loved to eat these, you know.''

"The cows?''

Another laugh. "Oh, yes, the cows. Twyman did love to eat. But I meant these,'' and she held out a sun-browned hand to show me three pellets. "Here, take one.''

It looked like a nugget of pressed wood.

"Eat it?'' I asked.

"Sure, its just compressed veggie stuff. Good for you. Like shredded wheat or oatmeal.''

I tentatively scraped my lower teeth over the two-inch pellet. A dry taste with an aftertaste of some kind of lettuce. I still preferred Twyman's taste in pies to the cow treat. I pocketed the nugget in my shorts.

"Ms. Medlock . . .'' I began.

"Clover.''

"Thank you. Clover, I was wondering what you could tell me about this.'' And I held out my hand with Twyman's very expensive diamond on it. It was easier to wear than stuff in my pocket.

The woman gave the ring a sideways glance as she pushed away the head of a black cow with a huge tumorlike sore covering its eye. "Need to call in the vet on this one again. Damn, every time I think I get it healed . . . Yes, I've seen that.''

"The ring?''

"Yes, Twyman showed it to me the night before he died. Tried to give the damned thing to me.'' Clover snorted as softly as the snuffling cow trying to get in the light canvas bag on her shoulder.

"Then it's yours,'' I declared, starting to take the ring off my finger.

"Oh, no, you don't. I don't want that thing. Wouldn't take it from him and won't take it from you.''

From Bondesky's picture, Clover Medlock had been a big, handsome woman. Big boned, with a smooth complexion and Scandinavian blond hair swept into a poufy bun on her head. Now, as she took off the Stetson to wipe a brow that finally acknowledged the heat of the high noon sun, I could see the hair had faded and was drawn up into a tight gray knot. With her long legs encased in faded jeans and a denim vest hanging loosely over the blue workshirt, it was no wonder I had first thought her a man. All of Clover's beauty now resided in her eyes surrounded by life's wrinkles. Lines around and above the mouth deepened with old disappointments as she pushed the ring away from her. She slammed the hat back on her head, shading her best remaining feature from the sun.

"Too little. Too late," she muttered as she headed on down the field, stirring up a myriad of shining insects with each step toward a stream banked with scraggly brush. "Watch where you step," she admonished as I followed her.

"Then what do I do with the ring?" I protested as I did indeed watch my step, sidestepping that which Clover had indicated in her warning. Only to wind up in another pile of it.

She scooted on down the slight incline toward the trickling water. "Keep it."

"Its yours," I insisted.

"Then if it's mine, I give it to you." She smiled her crinkly smile.

"No, I couldn't accept it. I just found it."

"Then throw it away. Give it away. Give it to *them.*"

I stared at where she pointed. "The cows?"

"Yes, the cows. I mean, no. Not these cows. Their counterparts." And the old eyes lit with mischief.

"Pardon?"

"You know about Twyman and his other wives?" she asked.

"Well, yes. But mostly from the news."

"So, meet them in person. Honey, meet Gabriella, Marcie, and Babe."

Three of the black and white bovines had followed Clover down to the water, including the only one I recognized, the one with the sore eye. Clover followed my eyes. "Babe," she said.

I grinned. Babe had been Twyman's last wife. The glamorous Hollywood movie star. This was humor I could understand. "And the Clover cow?" I asked.

Clover smiled back at me with an acceptance that had been missing before. "They're over there." She indicated two that had come down the other side of the small gorge.

"Both of them are Clovers?"

"Yep, I was the damned fool who married him twice, remember? And the stupid old fool thought I was up for grabs for a third go round. Some people never learn. But I did. Told him where he could put that ring," she snorted.

"He asked you to marry him two days ago?" I asked, really trying to sort it all out in my mind.

"Begged me, actually," she said with a self-satisfied little smirk showing on the left side of her mouth.

"Wow."

"Ayup. Waited many a year to tell him off. Almost made up for everything. Not quite, but almost. Took me almost a lifetime, but almost made up for . . .'' Her voice trailed off. "This is where we met, you know?"

"Here? On the ranch?"

"The ranch? You thought *this* was the ranch? Oh, Honey, honey." Then she added in an afterthought, "Bet you have hell with that name."

"If you only knew." I laughed. "But what do you mean? This isn't the ranch?"

"Oh, lord, no. This is just an old pasture. Well, where I had the first ranch. Doesn't even connect with mine now. I keep it for sentimental reasons. And for the girls." She nodded toward the five cows who were elbowing each other to get a sip from the thin stream.

Clover gestured back toward the assortment of rusty bars and gates. "This is where I was, that day when I met Twyman. Had a small herd, was just beginning to crossbreed." She added modestly, "Beginning to make a small name for myself.

"We were doing inoculations. Yearly vaccinations for the cattle. Had a few cowhands helping me out. Hot, like it is today. Twyman came driving up. Parked there." She pointed out the same spot where my Plymouth Voyager gleamed in the sun. "Had on a three-piece suit. Didn't even loosen his tie. He was a tall man, handsome." She looked to me for affirmation.

"Yes, I could tell," I agreed. And he had been, too. Despite the extra weight of both pounds and years, I could see where some women would think he held a certain charm.

"Well, sir," she said, sounding like Bondesky now. "He came wading through those cowpies without a second look down. I'm sure he had to throw away those city shoes afterward. Said he was from the Weatherford paper and wanted to do a local color story on me. Story about the little cowgirl who was making news with breeding. Hell, I was big then." She glanced at me. "Strong big. Farmgirl type, you know?

"That's when he ate his first cow treats. I give them to each cow after their shots to make them forget. Don't know if it does, but it makes me feel better about those big needles. Came and stayed, he did.

"I had arranged a barbecue for the hands. And some neighbors. We all helped each other out back then. Ate his fill, did Twyman. Liked his food."

I could attest to that.

Clover went on. Like it was a testimonial or eulogy.

"We sat on the bench at the table and he interviewed me. Then we started talking about writing."

I interrupted. "You're a writer, too?"

She went on like she hadn't heard me, but there was a subtle shift in her tone.

"Smooth talker, that Twyman. Yes, sir, good you're here, Honey. You were with him when he died. It's proper you're here now."

"Excuse me?" I didn't follow the lead of the conversation.

Clover unzipped the black fanny pack she had around her waist. I hadn't seen it because of the pellet bag. "The girls and I are glad you're here today." And she began to distribute another feed from the waist pack. Only she threw the gray powder into the air, watching as handfuls drifted into the creek.

The girls never missed a lick; their long pink fat tongues lapped up the silty water, ashes and all.

Ten

"Silas," I fairly screamed into the cell phone as I did my usual *get lost* maneuvers out of the country; drive a few miles, turn around in the middle of the road and drive the other way until I found another road. It was like a recipe; stir, make wrong turn, add eggs, turn left, add milk, go back the way you came, etc.

"Silas," I screamed again. "She cremated him."

Ever the patient detective, he said, "Yes, well, it was her right to do so, Honey. She claimed the body."

"But, but . . . she spread him out right there in

front of me. Fed him to the cows." I shivered with the memory. And rubbed the diamond ring against the seat of the van, trying to remove the powdery fingerprint Clover had left on the surface of the ring when she had said again, "You keep this, Miss Honey."

I was calming down, especially since I was finally steering toward the distant downtown outline of Fort Worth. "How come Clover got to claim the body? They're not married anymore."

Silas Sampson's voice faded in and out as I drove toward the source of his voice. "Honey, no one else wanted it. There was no next of kin."

"Okay," I said, accepting the fact, "but what about dead on Wednesday and flung out on Friday? Seems awfully fast to me."

"It *wasn't* murder, remember, Honey. Natural causes. You said so yourself."

"Now I'm not so sure."

"What? Honey, where are you? Can you meet me for a late lunch?"

"I'm at the corner of silver bridge and turn right, Silas. But I'm heading your way."

He laughed. "What would be your guess for an ETA for a late lunch at Massey's?"

I saw a sign that said To I-20. With probably only

two more wrong turns, I figured I could make it in about twenty minutes. We made a date.

Where Silas had poo-pooed my hysteria, Janie gloried in the description of the bucolic cowside ceremony in which I had unwittingly participated. Although she was farther away than Silas, her voice came in loud and clear. "Oh, man. Cool. Wish I had been there." Sometimes I have trouble remembering Janie is in her fifties.

"Okay, Honey. Give me an educated guess. Could she have done it?"

Knowing exactly what Janie meant, I mused, "She was bitter enough. Does that count?" I added, "And yet there was some sense of loss, like when she told me about their early years. How they met. I'll have to think about it. Weigh it out."

Right before I made the correct turn onto I-20, I caught my last glimpse of outback Fort Worth. Silhouetted against the huge sky that belongs to Texas, I saw a man with a plow being pulled by a mule. In this day and age of John Deere, it was an incongruous image, especially since the view from the left window revealed the familiar towers of Fort Worth standing tall against the same vast sky.

I turned toward the city skyline, but my inward eye was burned by the image of a stooped old man

with reins slung lightly over his shoulder, tilling the
ground of a sun-parched field. The dual images were
disturbing. I knew it had something to do with me,
my life, but I didn't know what.

Eleven

My mother had not been a good cook. Oh, everything was balanced—starches, protein, green stuff—but they didn't always make up into appetizing combinations. We ate out a lot. Reckon that's why I like restaurant food so much.

One of our favorite places to eat was Massey's over on Eighth Avenue. It broke my heart when they closed last year. Since they reopened a while ago, I hadn't had a chance to do an expert taste test, so I was glad that was where Silas and I were meeting for lunch. He knows how much I like chicken-fried steak. He ought to. He brought me enough carryouts when I found Steven Miller dead in my living room and wandered through a few days in shock. Silas may not be the sharpest detective in the world, but he was the first person to call on me socially since my parents died. Well, investigating a kinky, threatening phone call might not be considered a social visit by Amy Vanderbilt's standards, but it sure changed my life.

I could tell right off, when I drove up, that they were back to their previous quality: the parking lot was full of cop cars. They're better than truckers in giving their nod of approval for good food.

Everything seemed as usual. The place was packed. I could see Silas's blond head over a booth in the nonsmoking side, so I bypassed the waitress and headed that way. Just in time to hear Silas do a silly imitation of an old Nestlé's commercial. "Chock-lit," he croaked to the pretty little waitress. Well, now I knew he was telling her that we wanted chocolate pie for dessert, reserving it before they ran out, but, lord, I didn't know he flirted with waitresses.

"Make it two," I said as I slipped into my side of the new black booth. I looked around to see what else they had changed. Not much, I was glad to see. Oh, well, unless you count the plastic car seat at the entrance. I always envied the kids who bounced around on that old seat while they waited for a table, but I knew what my mother's disapproving sniff toward those rowdy kids meant. They do still have the sepia print of the 1940s though: my father's car is one of those shown parked outside the restaurant—a '41 Dodge. He used to show it to me every time we ate there.

The girl took her glue-stuck eyes away from Silas and gave me the once over. Not seeing much competition, she just asked me, "And what are y'all having to drink?"

"Me'll be having iced tea, thank you."

She sniffed and left.

I sang out the spelling of Nestlé just so Silas would know I had gotten his joke. Big oaf didn't even have the grace to blush. He very seriously said, "I was afraid they would run out. Would you look at this crowd?"

"You're looking good, Silas. Noticed on television last night that you had your hair styled."

Now he blushed.

"My regular barber was out . . . so . . ."

"Looks good," I reassured him as he nervously ran his hand over the full blond sides of his hair.

Did, too. Don't know why we have never connected.

Silas must have ordered my lunch, too, because

when Linda (I sneaked a peek at her nametag) brought us the iced tea, she also juggled two chicken-fried lunch specials on her arms. How do they do that?

Then she brought the mile-high chocolate pies out. That reminded me of Twyman eating his pie first. I put an admonishing hand on Silas's as his fork reached to scoop out a chocolate bite. "Don't. Trust me. Don't."

He looked puzzled, but only for a second, his fork already moving to cut into the steak. Yep, it's that tender at Massey's.

We paid serious attention to our food, pausing only to butter a yeast roll. It took several stuffings of chicken-fried steak mixed with cream gravy and fried potatoes in our mouths before we satisfied our first hunger cravings. Smiling, and waving his fork full of steak around, Silas said, "They'rrrrre baaaaack."

"Thank God," I sighed. "I've about killed myself all over Texas looking for good chicken-fried steak. I can't wait to tell Steven Hyatt." After Mother became so ill, Steven Hyatt used to join Father and me for dinner. I realize now that Father had been looking out for Steven's welfare, making sure he got enough to eat. The aunt he lived with hadn't been any better cook than my mother. Funny how you don't know things when they are going on, just when you're grown up. I'm trying so hard to grow up. I figure when I reach thirty, I'll just about know it all.

"Ah, yes, Mr. Hyatt. How is he, anyway?"

"Good. Good. Talked to him yesterday. Tried to tell me it was time I settled down. Quit running around all over Texas." I stifled a very unladylike snort. "Imagine the nerve. Mr. Tumbleweeds-for-Legs telling *me* to settle down."

"Well, he has a point, Honey. Better that than taking up a career chasing after bodies."

I ignored that statement and asked a question of my own.

"Which reminds me, Silas. Tell me about Twyman."

"I don't know why you are so all-fired suspicious of his death, Honey. Cut and dried. Cut and dried."

"Yeah? How so?"

He wiped his mouth with his napkin. "Big man. Big appetite. Bad heart. Diabetic. Stressful lifestyle." He repeated, "Cut and dried."

"Diabetic? I didn't know that," I mused. "He should have known better. Ate his pie first, Silas."

We both looked at the chocolate fantasy waiting for us.

"Cut and dried, hmmm? No autopsy? No inquiry?"

"No reason for it, Honey. Doctor signed the certificate and family didn't ask for one. Wouldn't have shown anything different," he asserted. "You could tell," he went on, "after they wiped those mashed potatoes off his face. Classic heart attack."

"What family, Silas? I thought you said he had no next of kin?"

"Well, that was a little sticky," he agreed. "We had to call all his ex-wives to find one that would claim the body. Went right down the line, backwards, and finally got Clover Medlock to do the right thing."

"How did they sound? Those ex-wives? When you told them about Twyman dying?" I wanted to know.

He bent his head forward so I knew he was going to tell me something he shouldn't. "They didn't give a rat's ass. Excuse my language. One of them even laughed."

"Get out of here. Laughed? Which one?"

"The foreign one. Gabriella something."

"Yeah, she was his second wife. Laughed, huh?"

Silas was kind. "Probably just a nervous reaction." He was into the pie now.

"Still . . . ?" I questioned.

"Happens all the time, Honey. First reaction sometimes. I tell you one thing though: Those women don't like each other one bit. Each one referred us to the next. That Babe even said, 'Why don't you call one of his other cows?' Now, that's harsh, Honey."

I gave him an appropriate grimace, but I was thinking about Clover and the "girls."

As Silas took the check and a wink from Linda, I said, "Still and all, Silas, I wish there had been an autopsy."

Silas stood up, growing tall in his official capacity. "It's over, Honey. I realize it was an unsettling experience for you. And coming so close on the recent deaths in your life, but it's over. Let it go."

We made our way to the parking lot, me clutching my carry-home box of pie. My eyes are always bigger than my stomach.

I fingered the ring on my hand. Silas hadn't even noticed it. Some cop he was. "I hear you, Silas. Yes, I will do that. Let it go."

"You know," he said, "Steven Hyatt might be right. You need . . ."

Waving my hand and giving him a Linda wink, I drove off before he could finish telling me what to do with my life. Or before I told him that Clover had invited me to the real ranch for a visit.

Oh, I would let it go, all right. But, "Cut and dried." Cut and dried?

Hmmm, I didn't think so.

Twelve

I use my father's old room for my war room. The darkened, knotty pine walls gave me comfort and courage as I planned out my next week's work— planned out my life, actually.

When my parents died, I had sought solace in my father's room. Gradually, the walls gave me strength, and I began a plan. A plan of living.

My natural instincts are to drift through life, watching and observing. Mother used to say I was a lot like my Great Aunt Eddie. Aunt Eddie had obviously enjoyed watching others, letting their actions fulfill her needs. She had never married but

was an incurable romantic in her way. It was her
house I lived in. My parents moved there when Aunt
Eddie and her two maiden sisters grew old and de-
pendent. Father had added the third story onto the
house for Mother and him to live in, but all the
sisters had died before it was fully completed. Now
it stood alone in a neighborhood converted into doctors' offices, the wrought iron "widow's walk"
peaking some repressed fantasy in my father's life.

Knowing they wouldn't be around when I was
grown, my elderly parents had schooled me daily in
discipline and structure. Instead of resenting the re-
strictions these lessons provided, I carefully listened
and learned. One didn't slide down banisters. One
didn't shout and squeal when one's mother had the
headache. One didn't daydream her day away.

I sat down at my gunmetal gray desk and began
planning my next week. I had everything I needed
right there in the war room. A telephone, Rolodex,
file cabinets, and wardrobe. Keeping one's clothes
clean and separated by seasons on long metal racks
kept one organized. Also my bible was my Day-
Timer; without it, I wouldn't have made it through
the first year after Mother and Father died. I had
been at a complete loss of how to live my life without my parents. The Day-Timer told me what to do,
hour by hour and day by day, until I began to get a

grip on life. But even now, ten years later, I needed that reassurance of order in my life.

Today was Friday. Tomorrow I would pick up the cleaning and begin packing my bag for Houston. My client was actually in Clear Lake—outside of Houston—an independent bookseller who specialized in the Spanish translations I carried in one of my lines. Sunday, I would wash my hair and give myself a manicure while refreshing myself on the coming week's itinerary.

I sighed; my life sounded boring, even to me. But once I was on the road, away from the house, it would change. I would change. I would breathe the fresh, hot air of a Texas summer, let the miles take away the responsibility of being responsible. By the time I reached the hill country, I would be smiling, looking forward to Clear Lake and then on to meet Harry.

Harry owned Sandscript, a small bookstore on South Padre Island. A retiree—a very young retiree—from the British Naval Service, Harry was certainly not the first man with whom I had had a relationship. (I had gone through the obligatory boy-girl thing when my parents died. Not at the house, of course.) But it was the most mature and satisfying relationship I had experienced. And, of course, I loved his dog, Bailey.

I sighed again and began compiling the papers I would need for the next week into a manila folder.

While I was in the midst of these machinations, the telephone rang with a conversation that not only changed my plans but maybe the direction of my life.

I made my own telephone call to Janie to tell her. I would have called Steven Hyatt, but I wasn't speaking to him right now. "Get married, my foot," I muttered as I finally gave into a full-blown snort of disgust.

"Janie? Honey. I need some advice."

"And you called me?" She sounded thrilled.

I told her about the telephone call I had just received from my boss at Constant Books. How they at the home office had been considering my request for a lighter workload: my compromise for now having all that money and still wanting to work. "They've already hired someone for my south Texas circuit," I said.

She sounded as amazed as I felt. "Oh, no. What will *you* do?"

"They don't know yet. But I am definitely not going to Houston on Monday." No Houston. No Harry. No Bailey.

Janie immediately came up with the same thought. "What on earth will Harry think?"

I thought I knew. The last time I had seen him was earlier in the summer when he had shown up at my house to ask me to marry him, and he had walked into a gaggle of men in my backyard, one of them dead. This trip to South Padre was when I had promised him an answer. It would have to wait, and I was glad because I didn't know the answer, myself.

"This is serious stuff, Honey."

"I have an idea, Janie, but I'll understand if it's too much trouble or inconvenient."

"What?"

I tried not to sound like a little girl asking her mommy for help. "Can you come and spend the night with me tonight?" I knew Janie had not only Pages to consider, but also somewhere in her life she had a husband whose name I didn't know. I kept meaning to ask. Surely he answered to something other than *Him*?

"Of course I can. I'll get *him* to watch the store tomorrow."

Before I could get a chance to ask his name, she added, "And we can watch the CBS special on Twyman tonight. They're promoting it every five minutes. CBS has film on all his wives."

I asked dryly, "And his books, I assume? He was famous because of his literary genius, Janie."

"Lord, Honey, you sound like I think your mother must have sounded. Of course, his books, but the juicy bits will be his personal life. Maybe we can get a clue as to which one killed him."

For the third time in an hour, I sighed.

Thirteen

"What I don't understand," said Janie as I turned off the television set following the maudlin, sentimental tribute to Twyman's genius, "is how on earth the police department let this one get by them. Why no autopsy?"

"Silas explained that. The doctor signed the death certificate, called it natural causes."

"Correct me if I'm wrong," Janie continued, "but I thought in Tarrant County—and Arlington *is* part of Tarrant County—that there *had* to be an autopsy unless the deceased had been in the hospital for forty-eight hours or unless the deceased's personal physician signed the death certificate.'' Janie knew every county law in Texas, I think.

"Far be it for me to correct you, Janie. I have absolutely no idea what the law is. But I think because she *was* present when he died, that the formalities were kind of waived. They did contact his personal physician in . . . Where did they say he lived?''

"The Cayman Islands.''

"The Cayman Islands, yes. And, his doctor there said Twyman *did* suffer a heart attack, a mild one, some months ago. And that he *was* a diabetic,'' I reminded her.

"Hmmm . . .'' And she wrote some notes in her ubiquitous notebook. I remembered that notebook and its pages of clues that Janie had entered following Steven Miller's death. She wrote in a shorthand that only she could read. I looked over her shoulder.

"Who is Mrs. Take?'' I asked.

"Mistake. That really spells mistake. Like the one the police made. They didn't need a physician on the scene. They needed a crime-scene examiner. But,'' and she sighed as she put away the notebook, "that doesn't surprise me.'' She shared what I would have taken for an insider's viewpoint if I hadn't known better. "Ever notice, Honey, how many mistakes are made when someone famous dies? Remember JFK? And, more recently, poor Mother Teresa? Doctors nationwide were going ballistic about her body lying there on that slab. All those people coming by and kissing her feet. Not that she didn't deserve it, mind you. Bless her heart. But still and all . . ."

"Mother Teresa wasn't murdered," I said. "And customs are different in India."

"Ah ha!" Janie exclaimed in a Sherlockian tone, "you're admitting Twyman *was* murdered?"

I looked around my living room as if I expected a hidden microphone. I also lowered my voice. "Janie, yes. I really think he was."

"Because?" She could hardly contain her excitement.

"Because I saw the look in his eyes when he asked my advice about someone trying to kill him. And, oh, because something didn't *feel* right about those wives of his. And . . . and . . ." I searched for more motivations.

But Janie had latched onto my last inane reason. "Ah ha! You felt it, too?"

We both were quiet for a moment, remembering the hour special we had just seen.

The hastily put together tribute featured news clips, mostly ones that had aired before during the announcement of his death, but they had also included some current interviews with his many wives. Some taped that very day, but all of them having the women utter some words about Twyman's talent and his work.

CBS had followed Twyman's life and work chronologically with Clover Medlock going first. It had been strange, watching younger versions of both the woman I had met that morning and of the man who I had seen die on Wednesday. The old black and white film segments of the two had jerkily shown an attractive, happy, and healthy couple. Clover had never taken her eyes off Twyman, giving him a cow-eyed devotion worthy of "the girls."

He had written *For All the Wrong Reasons* while married to Clover. When she had been asked how it felt to be married to such a talent, the Clover I had met this morning, her confident, well-educated voice incongruous with the weather-worn face, had answered, "Twyman always did have an eye for good writing."

Janie and I both came out of our silent musing at the same time and said as in one voice, "That was a strange thing to say."

Janie went on, "Yes, especially since that was exactly what Gabriella Rusi said, too."

Gabriella had been a surprise to me; her unexpected dark Mediterranean looks camouflaging her age, which I knew had to be younger than Clover but older than the woman actually looked. She was an exceptionally beautiful woman, but it bothered me that there was absolutely no expression radiating from her black eyes. No life there at all.

But the ex-wife who had bothered Janie the most was Marcie. "She had a sweet face, but I just don't trust women who tell other women how to lose weight," she said.

"She saved Twyman's life, for heaven's sake, Janie. He would have died years ago if Marcie hadn't found him and gotten him into a nutritional program." I quoted from the television special we had just viewed.

"Honey, there's a difference in helping someone with a special diabetic diet and fooling fat ladies. Even if they do lose weight at her 'exclusive east Texas health spa,' I bet you they gain every pound back—and more—on their drive home."

I could tell Janie was projecting her own weakness for fast-food calories as she listed all the possible opportunities for indulging between Marcie's spa—The Bargello—in Jefferson and Dallas. "I'll bet there are ten McDonald's and eleven Waffle Houses on that stretch," she declared.

"You've been there?"

"No, but I've passed by. I've smelled the raw

carrots and celery from the highway. I bet the minute you drive up to that security gate, they search your car and take away your Hershey's, not to mention your cheese and cracker stash.''

We were still debating the merits of a controlled diet plan—way off the subject of Twyman's women—when the phone rang. We hadn't even gotten to Babe yet.

''It's Steven Hyatt,'' I said as I slanted the caller ID toward the lamplight. I don't know why I have so much trouble reading that thing.

''Tell him I said hi,'' Janie said.

''*You* tell him yourself. *I'm* not speaking to him.''

That didn't mean I didn't eavesdrop, though. Not that I had to. Janie kept relaying his side of the conversation. ''Steven says he knows Gabriella. They are in negotiations for her to be the publicist on his movie.'' She corrected herself as she responded to Steven's end of the conversation. ''*Your* movie.''

''It's not my movie. It's his. I just gave him some seed money, that's all.''

''He says she's a really strange woman, but a fantastic publicist. Has an appointment with her tomorrow. Shall I tell him that we think she might have killed Twyman?'' Janie didn't wait for an answer but spouted off to Steven Hyatt all the reasons we thought Twyman was murdered. Then the conversation changed, and she lowered her voice and muttered words like "uh-huh" and "maybe" with an "I think so, too" thrown in here and there. I straightened up the living room, pretending not to hear or care.

Finally, she ended the conversation with, "Well, let us know, okay?"

When she hung up, she began helping me clean up, picking up her popcorn bowl and Coke can. We puttered in silence for a few minutes before I asked, "Well?"

"Well, what?" she replied in fake innocence.

"What was all that about?"

"Steven?" Janie was really carrying this too far, I thought.

"Yes, Steven. What did he say?"

"You could have talked to him yourself, you know."

"What's he going to let us know about?" I fairly screamed at Janie, and I never ever scream at anyone. "And what was all that whispering?"

"Well," she said, sitting down on the green velvet chair, the Coke spilling its last drips into the unpopped kernels in the bowl, "he said he would look around tomorrow when he kept his appointment with Gabriella. Just in case he saw anything suspicious.''

''Oh, right. Like he would know something unusual. It's the normal stuff that throws him.'' I sniffed just like my mother said Aunt Eddie had sniffed when she had her nose out of joint. In disdain.

''And the whispering?'' I persisted.

Unexpected tears welled in Janie's blue eyes and spilled onto her round cheeks. ''I don't know why you two are arguing. I know you love each other. Why is it that people who love each other can't talk?''

I forgot all about the snacking mess and went over to hug Janie. ''Oh, honey,'' I said, using my name to comfort her, ''I didn't mean to get you upset. Steven and I are just squabbling. It's not the end of the world. Do you want me to call him back?''

''You do love him,'' she sniveled.

''Of course I do. He was my only friend before you.''

We did some sisterly/motherly hugging before we wound our way upstairs. Janie always stayed in my mother's old room. She loved the high head- and foot-boards of the oak bed. She ran an appreciative hand over the starched eyelet cover before folding it back. "We didn't even get to talk about Babe." She yawned as the last of the moisture dried in her sleepy eyes.

"Tomorrow," I reassured her as I headed toward my bedroom. "Twyman's not going anywhere."

Fourteen

In the middle of the night, I got up from my sleep-less bed and padded across the hall. I stood in the doorway in my long, thin cotton gown with the blue flower sprigs and called Janie's name. When I heard her muffled response, I said, "Janie. In case you wondered. I gave Steven Hyatt some money for his movie because I have lots of it. I found it in the walls of the house after Steven Miller died. That's what the murderer was looking for. I didn't know it was there—my father hid it for me—but I finally found it."

I straightened the twisted lace that served for

gown straps and went on, "It was in the pantry.
Well, of course, I never went there on purpose, so
it was a while before I found it. Steven Bondesky
is upset about the piano, and of course he's right. I
just haven't decided what to do."

I said, "The piano?"

"Yes, that's where the money is hidden now.
There's over four million dollars in it. Steven Hyatt
knows I have some money but not how much or
where it is." I paused. "Well, I guess that's it. I
just wanted you to know. I think I can go to sleep
now. 'Night." And I tiptoed back to my room, not
sure whether she had heard me or not.

I think I did hear her say, "Good lord." Maybe
she was saying her prayers.

Fifteen

When it's hard for me to go to sleep, it's always even harder for me to wake up. Mother used to have to drag me out of bed for school, but I was bright-eyed and bushy-tailed on Saturday mornings. That was when I was young, before I appreciated Saturday morning as a snuggle-in day. Today, I luxuriated in a sleep-induced smile as my body wriggled against crisp sheets and layers of colorful pillows. I hugged my favorite stomach pillow close as I felt waves of sleep sending me back to oblivion. The sound that had awakened me forgotten in anticipation of . . . I sat upright in bed. Was that the *piano* I had heard?

I didn't even grab my seersucker robe before I glided down the stairs.

What to my wondering eyes doth appear? I thought as I took in the scene before me. Janie, in her voluminous white cotton gown, sat on the piano bench; her head, arms, and shoulders sprawled across the open keyboard. She was sound asleep, but as she turned her head to one side, her ears played a chord. *That* was what had awakened me.

"Janie," I said. Gently.

She opened her eyes and stared at the aisle of keys before her. "What?"

"Whaaat? You're asleep at the piano."

She sat up and looked around. "I didn't mean to fall asleep." The imprint of two black keys made a furrow over her right eye.

I couldn't resist. "I didn't know you played the piano."

"Play the piano? Play the piano?" She was awake now. "No one can *play* this piano. Only about six keys make a sound."

"Well, you found them. Those six keys woke me up." I headed toward the kitchen. "May I ask why you are having a concert this morning?"

Janie yawned as she followed me into the kitchen. "Did you or did you not say in the middle of the night that there is money in the piano? I've been afraid to look."

The coffee was made, the pot almost empty, in fact. I poured a cup. Janie handed me her cup, and I poured cold coffee down the drain, refilling it with hot from what looked like the end of the pot. Janie loves making coffee in my perk pot. I handed the cup back to her along with the sugar shaker. "Four million dollars, yes."

"And you expected me to go back to sleep?"

"Of course. I did. I've gotten used to the money."

We took our steaming cups back into the dining room. "Show me," she said.

Wordlessly, I flipped the switch on the chandelier and raised the top of the big upright piano. Even on tiptoes, Janie couldn't peer over the top. She raised her gown above her knees and stepped up on the bench. "Holy Toledo," she gasped.

I closed the lid and helped her to the floor. We sat down at the table.

Holding her coffee cup in two hands, Janie took a big gulp and said, "So, you miss playing the piano?"

As straight-faced as she, I answered, "Not much. 'Beautiful Dreamer' was about all I could really ever master."

"Honey, you really do need a mother. That money has got to go. Today."

"I know. But . . . where?"

"How about a bank?"

I deadpanned back at her. "Right. And they won't want to know where it came from? I won't have to pay mega taxes?"

"Ever hear of safe-deposit boxes?"

"Ever see how little they are? Besides," I said as I got up to refill my cup, bringing the pot for Janie who waved it away with murmurs of "That's the third pot," "I want the money to grow."

"Oh, right. It's growing in there," she said as she gestured toward the upright. "Growing dust bunnies."

"I know. I know. But I've decided what to do with it."

"And . . . that is . . . ?"

"I'm going to give it all to Bondesky."

"Because? Honestly, Honey, this is like pulling teeth."

"Because he knows about the money and has *ways* of getting it into investments that I don't know about."

Janie snorted. "I would think he would, yes. Honey, it's called off-shore, black-market money laundering."

"Yeah? I wondered how he was going to do it."

"It doesn't bother you that it might be illegal?" she asked.

"Oh, really, Janie. Bondesky just looks illegal. I'm sure it will all be aboveboard. My father earned that money. I reckon if I have to pay a few taxes, I'll just have to pay a few taxes. Bondesky can handle all that. Where are you going?"

Janie paused at the doorway and sat her still-full cup on top of the piano. I'm going to call my husband and tell him I won't be there today. That I have to help you move . . . assets."

I grinned. "Yes, call . . . him. By the way, I've been meaning to ask you . . ." But she was already on the phone and waved me away.

I mimicked Janie by cradling my cup of coffee in two hands and staring at the piano over the rim. I was going to miss that money.

Sixteen

Before we got more than half the money loaded into garbage bags, the world shifted, and my life took another of those life-changing turns.

It started with the doorbell. It's always the door-bell when it's not the telephone.

Janie squealed when we heard the ring and sat her ample self on top of as many bags as she could, spreading her white gown over a few others. "Don't answer it. We're not home."

"Don't be silly. Let me see who it is." I peered around the door toward the hall where, through the glass door, I could see a woman reaching for the bell turner again. "Oh, my, it's Ms. Patton."

"Patton?"

"No," I corrected. "Potter."

"Potter?"

"Yes."

Janie was getting good at screaming at me. "Who is Ms. Potter?"

"Bondesky's secretary. Wonder what she wants?" I headed toward the door as Janie assumed a diva-on-the-couch look, leaning way back to hide more bags.

I opened the door a crack. "Yes? Good morning."

"Miss Huckleberry? Is that you?"

I opened the door a little wider to show it was me. "How can I help you, Ms. Potter?"

"Well, I ordinarily don't work on Saturdays, but I was in the office for a few minutes this morning and when the packages arrived, I thought I would just pop over and bring them to you. Did I *wake* you?" she asked in a voice that indicated that I was a major sleep offender.

"No, of course not. I was just . . . I mean, I got into doing some housecleaning and haven't taken the time to dress. It's so nice of you to bring the packages." I added, "What packages?"

Ms. Potter beamed. "Your computer. It came this morning."

"Wonderful. Just leave it right there. Thank you."

She smiled that superior Ms. Potter smile. "No, you don't understand. I'm here to put it together for you and show you how it works. Oh, and your dog is here in the taxi."

I shook my head to clear it.

"I don't have a dog in a taxi."

Same smile "You do now."

Looking beyond her oh-so-very-managed hair, I saw a white taxi at the curb, parked behind Ms. Potter's sensible sedan, the driver unloading a hard plastic crate. "There must be some mistake," I said.

"No, I checked and verified the address for you. Would you like me to see to it?" Her blue eyes indicated one didn't talk to taxi drivers in one's gown.

I could hear Janie moaning from the dining room.

"Here's the paperwork that accompanied the dog." And she handed me a large manila envelope. It was addressed to me. From Harry.

"Please," I said in defeat. I took the envelope from her.

As she clicked her heels down the sidewalk to the taxi, I tore it open. Several pieces of typed papers and one handwritten note slid out. I read the note first.

Honey,

Sorry I haven't been able to get you on the phone. The timing is lousy, but I have an emergency in London. Mother is ill. Rosa is looking after Sandscript but couldn't take Bailey. Didn't know whom else, so you've got him. Just have time to make connection.

Will call. Thanks . . . I love you.

Harry

I sat down on the first step of the stairs. "Oh, great," I sighed.

"What is it, Honey?" Janie yelled from the improvised bank vault area.

"Can you spell *pandemonium*, Janie?"

Actually, it wasn't all that bad.

While I retrieved my robe from the bedroom, Ms. Potter and the taxi driver got Bailey uncrated and in the house. He met me halfway up the stairs like his only long-lost relative, relieving himself on the third newel post in what had to be anxiety, pleasure, and a desperate need.

The taxi driver assured us he had been well-paid and left us with the dog and the carrier, after Ms. Potter had given him an extra tip to take the multiple computer boxes up the stairs to the war room.

Janie refused to budge from the garbage bags when I made introductions but was gracious and smiling all the same. "Just helping Honey out with some housekeeping," she said. Bailey loved Janie at first sight. On the second sight, his big golden head started tearing open the bags. Thankfully, Ms. Potter had already sniffed an Aunt Eddie sniff and was on her way back to the war room. I followed her, shrugging my shoulders and spreading my hands wide in helplessness as Janie pulled hundred-dollar bills from Bailey's mouth. "Good dog. Good dog. Want some water? Toast? Caviar? You seem to have expensive taste." Bailey slobbered bills and followed her into the kitchen.

Like I said, it wasn't all that bad.

Later, when I had dressed in jeans and a T-shirt, I rejoined Janie and Bailey downstairs. Ms. Potter was efficiently pulling hardware out of the boxes and following the color-coded schematic to connect the computer cables. She seemed happy to be left alone to her own devices, so I did.

Bailey was chewing on a full box of Pop Tarts and also seemed happy.

I sat down beside him on the floor and hugged his neck. I was trying to figure out what to do with the money on a Saturday.

Janie was continuing to stuff bags with money.

"Honey, you lead such an exciting life. Everything would just be perfect if we could figure out who killed Twyman."

I scratched Bailey behind the ears. I know nothing about dogs. I know nothing about investments. I know nothing about computers. Today, murder was at the bottom of my list. "Twyman?" I asked.

Seventeen

I may have forgotten about Twyman, but Bondesky, strangely enough, had not.

"So how's the murder investigation going, Huckleberry?" was what he wanted to know as we unloaded the bags of money from my van. "You any closer to figuring out who done it?" It was half a joke and half serious. It kind of reminded me of when Twyman had asked me for help.

"Why do you ask, Bondesky?"

He was out of breath from hoisting the money, so he panted like Bailey when he answered, "Just curious. You're good at that sort of thing. Just wondered what was going on."

I don't know much about murders and mysteries, but Janie has taught me one thing. When someone asks a question or behaves in a different manner, something's going on. My wrong accusation of murder had once put Bondesky behind bars for a while. Somehow, I didn't think that in his mind that qualified me for being good at investigating.

So I asked again, "Why do you ask, Bondesky?"

He pulled the last of the improvised money bags into his office and collapsed into his desk chair. I responded to the waving motion of his hand by rummaging in his new executive refrigerator and popping open a bottle of Evian for him. Then I took one for myself. Money running is a tiring affair.

"How much money did you keep out?" he finally managed to say.

"Enough. Why are you not answering my question?"

Bondesky downed the second bottle I placed in front of him. He looked like he could have stood to have one poured over his head, too, but I resisted.

"Well, it's like this." He grinned that sly grin that people do—along with the eye thing—that lets you know you've caught onto them. "Someone asked me what you'd found out. That's all."

I did some mental calculations in my head. "Clover," I concluded.

"Well, yeah. She really liked you, Huckleberry."

"Does she think Twyman was offed, too?"

"Of course not," he said quickly. Too quickly.

I assumed my usual hip-on-the-desk position and drank my yuppie water. "Then how did you two happen to talk about me thinking Twyman was murdered?"

"It kinda came up."

"Right."

"Okay. Okay. It's like this, Huckleberry. She calls and she says you came out. Then she says why are you so interested in Twyman. I told her it was the ring, but she says she don't think so. So maybe I mention you like to investigate murders."

"Did she tell you about the cows and the ashes?"

"She might of mentioned them, yes."

"And did she tell you she didn't want the ring? Wouldn't take it, in fact?"

"Ayup."

"And does she think Twyman was murdered?" I didn't think so, but I asked anyway. If Clover had suspected foul play, she would have requested an autopsy. Wouldn't she?

"Nah. She doesn't think the guy was murdered. But she wonders why you do."

I changed the subject. "What are you going to do with the money, Bondesky?"

"Awww, put it here. Put it there. Don't worry about the money, Huckleberry."

That's all I wanted to know about the piano money. I knew the old fellow would take good care of it and it would come back twofold at least. If there were taxes or penalties to pay, he would take care of them. What I know about finances would fill a thimble and leave room for the Sphinx.

"I like Clover," I finally said.

"Like I said, it was mutual. She maybe wants you to call her again."

"Maybe I will. I need some advice. I'm into livestock now." And I told him about Bailey.

"*Now* you get a watchdog." He laughed. "You always were an after-the-barn-door-closed type of person, Huckleberry."

"She really wants to see me again?" I knew Bondesky's offhand comment to that effect was more urgent than the delivery had been.

Having delivered the message, Bondesky relaxed. I could see him touching the top of his head, looking for the discarded eyeshade. He was ready to get back to business. Social banter wore him out. "Sure, give her a call."

Then he did a funny thing. Looked around like

Ms. Patton/Potter was still in the outer room and lowered his voice. "Let me give you this one, Huckleberry. Ask her about the book."

"What book?"

"That *For All the Wrong Reasons* book; that's the book."

"Tell me," I begged.

But he was through confiding.

I turned over the thought in my head. What on earth did Clover want to tell *me* about the book? The one that Twyman had written when he was married to her? Out loud, I said, "Thanks for sending Ms. Potter over this morning. She is very efficient and a good teacher. Had my first lesson on the computer."

"Yeah? How'd that go? You a whiz now?"

"Well, I know how to turn it on. How to play solitaire. And I printed out a letter addressed to someone I don't know. Yeah, I think I'm a whiz. Just have one question."

"What's that?"

I pointed to the white object he held in his hand, ready to go to work when I left. "They don't really call this a mouse, do they?"

Eighteen

I am now a solitaire whiz.

I didn't do the laundry. I didn't eat. I fed the dog and fondled the mouse the rest of the weekend. I think Bailey used my mother's carpet for a lawn, but hey, I got to watch the dancing cards tell me *hurray* when I beat the game. Good thing I don't smoke. I am a closet addict.

"Steven, I have lost my soul," I told Steven Hyatt about noon on Monday when he called. "What day is it?" I had forgotten I was not talking to him—even forgot to give unknown poet's lines. Oh, lord, had I said good-bye to Janie? Was Janie gone?

"Help me," I pleaded to Steven.

He lied and said, "You'll get over it. I once was a Microsoft Solitaire champion, myself. I'll send you the hard stuff."

"Oh, gee, thanks. Just what I need. It has cleared my head a little, though. You can think when you're not thinking. Steven, I'm sorry I was such a horse's patootie last week." I really have to expand my vocabulary. Surely there are other words. "I'm trying to remember why I was angry at you."

"I told you to get a life, not an obsession."

"Oh, yeah. Marriage. Was that a proposal, Steven?" I joked.

"Not yet, Honey."

I laughed.

"I called to tell you about my visit with the one and only Gabriella."

"Ah, the second Mrs. Towerie. How'd that go?"

"Strange, strange woman, Honey."

"Tell me."

I didn't know I was still playing solitaire while talking to Steven until he said, "I will if you take your hands off that mouse." How did he know?

"Done," I lied.

"Liar."

He knows me so well.

"Never mind. I won't tell you that she is broken up over Twyman's death. *Not*. Or that she sneered when I mentioned his name while offering my sincere condolences. You don't get to hear that then I did some sleuthing for you."

This time I did let go of my new rodent friend. "Yeah? How so? What did you find out?"

"Ah ha! Thought that would get you. Actually, I'm not sure what I found out. Does the word *Bargello* mean anything to you?"

"Sure, that's the name of Marcie's health spa." The "girls" were becoming first-name people in my mind. Well, cows, anyway. Whenever I heard their names, I thought of which cow had what name. Gabriella had been the dark one. I was beginning to see Clover's logic in the naming.

"Yes, I remember now. From the television special. That's why it seemed familiar."

I didn't reply. Steven often tells more when he's rambling than when he's questioned.

Sure enough, he went into a long, detailed explanation of how he and Gabriella were looking at papers—contracts—when she was called out of the room. His penchant for nosiness prevailed in those few short minutes. *He* called it intellectual curiosity. He did a song and dance about how he had shuffled the contracts over her desk, causing him to mix them up with some of her papers, forcing him to look at them carefully.

I picked up the mouse and clicked on New Deal. "Go on," I said.

"Somehow Gabriella's calendar printout was mixed up with my papers. I don't know how that happened. But I double-checked to make sure it wasn't my papers, and that's when I saw the name Bargello. On August eighth. Circled in red."

"Okay," I responded absently. You have to do that to keep Steven going. Like stepping on the accelerator in the car. A little more gas for another mile.

"Beside the circle were three names. Want to guess who they were?"

"Marcie, Clover, and Babe."

"Bingo."

I put the black queen on the red king. "Steven, I thought these women hated each other. How come they're doing a wife's reunion at Marcie's?" I glanced at my own calendar. August the eighth was three weeks away.

"Beats me," he said. "But it must be a big thing."

"Because?"

"Because when Gabriella came back—I had replaced the calendar by then—she grabbed it and turned it over. And she glared at me. Well, that wasn't unusual, she's a first-class glarer. But it was one of those questioning glares. You know?"

"Yes," another push on the gas.

"Like she was trying to guess whether I had seen anything. Read her calendar. Like she didn't trust me."

"Go figure," I said.

His verbal motoring had stopped. It was my turn to drive.

"Okay, this is what we have. Four ex-wives. One dead man. They all divorced him . . ."

"Or *were* divorced," Steven amended.

"Yes. I wonder if he left them or if they dumped him?"

"Good question."

"Well, I can find out about Clover, anyway. She wants to see me. Something about Twyman's first book," I told him.

"Interesting that you should mention his book. One of the things I told Gabriella was how proud she should be that he wrote *Down by the Riverside* when they were married."

"And what did she say?"

"Honey, it's funny, but I swear, I she looked frightened. She just muttered something about appreciation for my time and that she would get back to me.''

"Frightened? That *is* strange, Steven. Lord, wouldn't you love to be a fly on the wall when those women get together in August?'' I grinned at the thought.

"Another thing about that, Honey. Tell me why they are all going to The Bargello? Not a one of them is fat.''

"Goose, you don't have to be fat to go to a spa. It's like nutrition and good eating and living right.''

"No booze, eh?''

"Nope. Just mud baths and facials.'' I sighed. "And massages and pedicures and all those wonderful pampering things. Someday, when I am rich, I'm going to treat myself to a week at a spa.''

"Er, Honey?''

"Hmmm?'' I put the last king on the pile. The cards started their march of triumph across my monitor.

"Honey, you *are* rich.''

Nineteen

One of the first lessons I learned from my book rep mentor was to avoid at all costs the lure of fast food on the road. His name was Kantor, and he was a wee little Jewish man who could have made a good living in the 1890s as a drummer. There wasn't a rope he didn't know about the book business. That he was willing to show me the convoluted knots of his trade was a puzzle that he explained over a delicate lunch of trout almondine in this quaint restaurant in a small town in south Texas.

"Now, Miss Honey, they don't have a bookstore here in Buford, but when you're on the road, *food is king,''* he told me when they served us our lunch, the Tuesday special at LD's Eat and go. The Main Street café off the town's square would never have beckoned me through its doors without Kantor's guidance. Now it's a regular stop. Although I personally prefer Monday's meat loaf.

As we ate the Chocolate Surprise for dessert, Kantor told me, "Anyone can eat at McDonald's. In fact, over a million a day do. But," and he emphasized this remark with his fork, "they miss out on the adventure of getting to taste life." Kantor made the word *life* seem like a masterpiece of art. "Look around you. These are the real people of the world. So it takes an hour instead of fifteen minutes to eat. Would you ever see these wonderful faces? These stereotypes of humankind? These blessed souls?"

I often thought Kantor would have made a great Baptist evangelist.

As both my mother and my father had been restaurant people-watchers, making up tales about overheard snatches of conversation, I appreciated Kantor's affirmation of this idiosyncrasy.

Kantor was retiring, he told me over that first luncheon. He had purchased a plot of land in the Hill Country years ago, and with every trip south from Dallas where he lived, he would stop by and gaze at his land. He must have been nearly sixty when he decided looking wasn't enough. Now he lives in a prefab cabin overlooking a small pond. He dresses every day in one of his colorful, trademark vests complete with white shirt and tie and sits on his deck in a rocker, reading all the books he never had time for when he was on the road.

I drop by from time to time. Without his careful tutelage of the rules of the road, I would never have made it. My parents had died a few years before, I had finished at Tarrant County Junior College, and, of all the introductions to life I have received, I think I appreciate Kantor's the most. He never talked down to me. Never assumed I knew something I didn't. Never teased me.

Kantor loved his customers, knew everyone by first name, and would even take over the store if they called him. "Independent booksellers are the real heroes of the literary world," he would confide to me as we stopped at another client's store. "They don't make any money. They often have to borrow from the bank to pay the distributors. They are often eccentric, quarrelsome, and opinionated, but, ahhh, they love books. They know their authors, and they know their customers.

"They are happy to see book reps arrive like a postman on his appointed rounds. These mavericks of bookselling, abhorrers of chain bookstores, pore over the new catalogs like a child opening up the JCPenney Christmas catalog. They make their purchases very carefully, with an eye to the dollar amount. Profit before pleasure. Three of this one. Ten of that. Just one of the new author.

"We do a dance, these buyers and I. I show. I preen. I showcase. I demur." He sighed. "It's beautiful."

"Miss Honey," he admonished, "be a virtuoso of the road. Know your stock. Know your people. Never, ever let a Dairy Queen or Burger King sack sully your floorboards or back window. Oh, my dear, I'm leaving you a legacy of well-tended shops; treat each as if they were Harrods. Breathe deeply each time you enter the stores. Words, thoughts, ideas, and passions. That's what you smell in bookstores."

"Tell me again why you are leaving this utopia?" I wondered aloud.

"Computers," he had whispered in a hissing voice that often signaled the arrival of a villain on stage. "Computers will kill us all."

A bit dramatic, I'll admit. But that was Kantor.

And right on target.

For the first few years after I took over from Kantor—learned his route and charmed his customers—

I could still do it the old way. I whipped out catalogs and sold profits and dreams. I encouraged limited owners to expand their stock, assuring them there was life after best-sellers, and I discouraged those who tended to overbuy. I became a virtuoso.

Finally, the computer revolution caught up to me. That was why I had asked Bondesky's help with setting me up a system. So I could help my clients. This was the proposal I had sold Constant Books. It's amazing how brave you can be if you have money to back up your pitch. I would no longer just be on the road. I would be the systems adjuster for Constant, helping independents set up inventories on computers.

All I had to do was learn how to do it myself first.

After hanging up the telephone call from Steven Hyatt, I looked around my war room/office. In one corner, the shrouded hangers of my well-organized travel wardrobe hung expectantly. The file cabinets still exuded the confidence and professionalism I had worked so hard to achieve.

But at the corner near the window, the new queen reigned. The Dell special I had named Miss Mc-Gillicudy. And so entered chaos. On the floor, beside the missed target of the trash basket, lay no less than three identifiable sacks. Burger King. Taco

Bell. Jack-in-the-Box. I am happy to say that McDonald's made it all the way to the bottom of the can.

My eyes hurt. My back was beyond straightening. My arm was numb. My legs were dead. I was well on my way to becoming a computer nerd.

I pulled down my beloved Day-Timer. Its soft leather binding gave me a touch of reality. Tomorrow, my first computer assignment. In Jacksboro.

I paused. Jacksboro. Out where Clover had her real ranch.

Computer nerd. Private investigator?

I laughed as I turned to the page that held Clover Medlock's phone number.

Twenty

I was so tired when I pulled into Clover's driveway the next night that I thought I was going to die. It's strange to me that, now that I have all the money in the world, I am working harder than I ever have. "What's wrong with this picture?" I asked myself as I limped up the walk to the front door. There seemed to be a severed nerve between my back and my left leg. Right leg?

"Whoa, Bailey. I'm glad to see you, too. Just not so enthusiastic, please," I said as a hundred pounds of blond lab greeted me at Clover's open door.

"He missed you," she said as she pulled the dog off me.

"So I gather. Was he good?"

Clover had insisted that I bring Bailey by her ranch early in the morning before I hightailed it on to Jacksboro. I asked if she knew of a good kennel that would keep him for the day, but she said if I was coming back for supper, it would be no problem for her to take him on the ranch for the day.

I was surprised at Bailey's affection. We actually don't know each other that well, but I guess with Harry gone, I was the one familiar smell in his life. I guess. I don't know much about dogs. Mother had been allergic to them and I'd never had a pet, so I treat Bailey as I would a guest. As if I'd had very many of those, either.

It had not been that difficult to find Clover's ranch. Her directions had been clear and easy, even for a dysfunctional direction finder. It has always amazed me that two points on a map can actually be connected if one only has the right path. I hadn't driven far out of Fort Worth before I became aware of a flat vista of fences and scrub bushes interspersed with clusters of trailer parks, local beauty shops, and body garages. Body garages. Boy, what an image that stirred. I started singing have a leg, have an arm, have a head to the tune of "Have an Eggroll," Mr. Goldstone from *Gypsy*.

By the time I'd reached the first oil wells pumping away amid a few scattered cacti, the sun was beginning to rise, its first rays catching the night's dew in a sparkling array. The July sun would dry the drops quickly, competing with the thirsty ground for the sparse moisture. It hadn't rained since early spring. The clear blue sky indicated that today would be no different.

As Clover had stated, I had no problem recognizing her spread. The rest of the acreage might have been bone dry and brown, but the entrance to her ranch was an oasis of old green pecan and oak trees that wound past the stucco archway for several miles to the ranch house. Gnarled mesquite trees protected the perimeter of the taller trees before giving way to the scrub beyond. It was a well-planned progression of trees that tapered off into the beginnings of the harsh plains of a west Texas landscape.

The main ranch house was surrounded by the twisted mesquites with several weeping willows added to give an illusion of cool laziness. The house was actually a Mexican villa, complete with a tiled fountain spurting water into a dry air that would absorb most of it before it had a chance to splash back into the basin. A red-tiled overhang held baskets of impatiens and fiesta bright portulacas, and earthen pots of more impatiens and a few cacti surrounded the front doorway. I knew it had taken big bucks to create the casual, colorful entrance. Guess there was money in them there Branguses.

When we settled Bailey down, I followed Clover through the house and out into another courtyard, landscaped as the entrance was, creating the illusion of a cool summer evening. I sighed as Clover thrust an icy margarita in my hand. Tan wicker fans revolved above me, hanging from the slanting roof of the overhead and creating an additional illusion of a breeze.

"This is exactly how I would live if I were a rancher," I said approvingly.

"Thanks," Clover replied as she sat in an accompanying wicker chair, a margarita in her hand also. With the boots she had worn this morning replaced by woven huaraches, I could see her wriggling her toes, which encouraged me to slip out of my sandals and slide my own feet across the cool brick of the patio floor. My toes played with the thick mat of closed portulacas that crept between the bricks.

All my friends seem to be old. Of course, it's no wonder I get along with older people. Look at my upbringing. But somewhere along the way, I should have acquired a contemporary girlfriend or two. The woman I worked with today qualified for the age bracket, but I wasn't sure where the relationship was going.

I told Clover about my day after she politely asked.

"Juliana has a tough job ahead of her," I shared. "She knows less about the book business than I know about computers. Together, we had fun," I admitted. "She inherited the bookstore from her aunt. Papyrus is a good little store, but Jacksboro is just not that big. Sorta like my friend Janie owning Pages in West. If either of them really needed the income from sales, they'd be starving."

"Well, it's the only bookstore I know around here," said Clover. "New books, I mean. McMurtry's place over in Archer City carries used books—every book ever printed, I think." She smiled. "Ever been there?"

"No, but it's on my list of places to visit. Up to now, south Texas has been my territory. I'm just learning about west Texas."

"How do you go about setting up a computer inventory?" Clover asked as if she were really interested.

Good question. "The program is self-explanatory. Plug it into the computer and fill in the blanks. After

that, it's a matter of constant maintenance of sales
and receivables. But the getting there is something
else." I took a sip of my sweet/sour drink. "I heart-
ily recommended to Juliana that she call in all her
friends and family for an inventory party. A week-
long party." I grinned.

"With you helping out?"

"Oh, yes. That's the plan. Constant wants me to
be a part of the process. It doesn't cost them much
in the way of my services and will eventually boost
sales. Or so they say." All in all, I hadn't embarrassed myself too badly. Ms. Potter was a good
teacher. I made a mental note to call and thank her
as well as ask about some questions that had come
up during the day.

We sat that way, talking about books and munch-
ing on chips and salsa, letting the day fade and
the night take over. When the stars began to fill the
skies, an older woman came out and replaced the
chips with hot plates of homemade Mexican food.
To taste real refried beans and onions cannot be de-
scribed. Nor the spicy beef enchiladas. Clover
seemed as hungry as I was, although I had eaten
two hamburgers for lunch at Herd's in Jacksboro.
It's a third-generation hamburger shack, and each
burger is individually made to order. How could I

not eat two? Someday, I figure, all this pigging out will catch up to me.

Instead of coffee, we enjoyed frosty glasses of mint iced tea after our meal. I couldn't move. Could not move if my life depended on it.

So Clover had me at a disadvantage when she finally got down to the questions she wanted to ask me.

"I understand from Steven that you think Twyman was murdered. May I ask you why you think so?" she asked after the help had cleared the table.

She seemed older tonight. More wrinkled. Not as strong.

I didn't want to tell her about Twyman asking me about someone trying to murder him, but I did. Homemade tortillas go a long way in loosening my tongue.

Clover laughed. "Are you sure he didn't say, trying to do him in? Or do a number on him?"

"Why, no," I said in surprise. "He definitely said *kill.*"

Clover snorted with no ladylike reservations. "Shoot, Honey, if anyone was in any danger of being killed, it was me."

"You?"

"Yep. Do you recollect that I told you he came

out here with that ring? That one you tried to give
me? Asking me to marry him for the third time?''
She slapped her blue-jeaned thigh in laughter.

"Yes," I replied cautiously.

"Yep," she said again. "See, he had found out.
Can't imagine how. But he had. That I was writing
this book. This memoir.'' She snorted again. You've
really got to admire that habit. With Clover it was
a real art form.

"A book about him?"

She nodded. "Scared the pee out of him, it did."

"You write?"

"Do I write? Oh, my yes, honeychile, I write."
This snort surpassed the others, almost choking Clover in the process.

"Oh. I didn't know that. Are you published?"
Anyone can write, I have discovered. Published is
another affair.

This question all but sent her to the floor of the
brick patio.

Wiping her eyes with the back of her hands, the
tiredness I previously noticed seemed wiped away
also. The subject of Twyman and the book seemed
to revitalize her. "Oh, my, yes. In a manner of
speaking, I am published.''

"Would I have read you? What book? Or is it

books?" I searched my internal computer list for a Medlock title.

Clover gave me a sly look. "You'll have to wait and find out."

"Wait for the memoir, you mean?"

She gave me a close-lipped, sprightly grin in answer.

"Would he really have killed you to keep his past quiet? I don't understand. Everyone knows about his marriages. His life is an open book. No pun intended," I apologized.

"You think?"

The stars were shining brightly overhead. I felt a real breeze begin somewhere beyond where the trickling water of a fountain waterfall played a lulling tune. The warm air, the drinks, and the food had left me in a stupor. I yawned. And apologized.

The last thing I remember was the older Mexican woman leading me into a side door from the patio, Bailey following behind. The narrow wooden bed with its serape cover was as inviting to him as it was to me. We fought over the pillow, and I lost.

Twenty-One

Because I had enjoyed an unintentional sleepover at Clover Medlock's ranch, the next day was thrown off-kilter. I thought about throwing my Day-Timer out the window and just living one day at a time, but old habits die hard, so I spent a few minutes rearranging the lists I had prepared for the day. I still went back to Jacksboro, in a T-shirt that proclaimed Brangus Reigns, but Juliana was so happy to see me that she never noticed. I do try to look a little more professional than I did.

I showed her how to enter ISBN numbers in the computer, marking each book entered with a Post-it note and reshelving them. She looked at the crammed shelves and asked, "And I have to do that to all of them?"

"Yes, and put in the author's name, the title, and cost."

"Honey," she wailed, "that's a lifetime job."

"I'm going to ask Constant to send you a bar code reader. That should speed up the process. In the meantime, it will be good for you to know the routine." God, I sounded so self-righteous. Imagine me, telling someone else how to live her life.

The big variant of the day had been a stop for dinner at Café 1187, where I met with Clover and Bailey. She had been so gracious to keep him another day.

We left him in my van while we had shepherd's pie and iced tea. The owner and chef brought us lemon chess pie for dessert without my having to order it. She knew it was my favorite.

I had met Michelle just as I meet most people on the road. I had stopped to ask for directions and found myself another favorite on-the-road restaurant worthy of Kantor. There's a stable next door, the Currah Riding Stable, and Clover soon was talking horses with the Irish owners. Only the right dining room was open, and it was crowded with horsey people and locals as well as one couple who had driven out from Fort Worth for dinner. I was glad to see the customers. I don't know why I worry about local restaurants just as much as I do independent bookstores. Guess I have a fear of the popular edging out the individuality of the world.

Bailey collected and Clover paid back for her hospitality, I headed on into Fort Worth. I meant to stay on 377 but wound up turning off on I-20 East, so it was almost dark when I arrived home. Dark came late on July nights, so it was still light enough for me to see a car parked in front of my house.

I recognized it as Janie's, and, sure enough, she was sitting in my front porch swing, her short legs barely grazing the wooden porch floor.

"Did I miss something?" I said in greeting. I didn't remember scheduling her for a visit tonight, but I knew my Day-Timer was screwed up. I bit my tongue and added, "Janie, I'm glad to see you."

She was as unmannerly as I had been. "You're late, and I'm hungry."

Confused, I asked, "Were we supposed to have supper together?"

"No. I just took a chance . . . and when you weren't home . . ." She burst into tears. "Oh, Honey, I've done it. I've left him. I've run away from home."

Now I guess I don't ever have to find out his first name.

I patted the woman in the swing as I have learned to do to Bailey. It calmed her as it does him. I guided her inside and fixed a supper of bacon and eggs. She told me as much as she ever was going to. It was about what I had thought. A relationship that had pretty much petered out. After her first burst of emotions—and with a full stomach—Janie forgot to be dramatic about her seemingly impulsive but actually long-thought-out decision and was more eager to know about my visit with Clover.

I helped her unload the luggage she had brought with her. That she would stay was an unspoken given. "Janie, I really like Clover. I'm dying to read her memoir. She says that's what got Twyman so agitated. Why he accepted the Arlington Library's invitation to speak. And why he was muttering about murder."

"Do we still think he was murdered?" she asked.

"Yes, I do. Clover was acting a bit too coy not to know more than she said. And believe me, Janie, Clover is not a coy person."

We moved her stuff into the sleeping porch off Mother's room and chattered more about the mystery of Clover's book while we prepared for bed. With Bailey walked for the last time for the evening and Janie under Mother's coverlet, I finally curled up in the wad of pillows of my own bed and

stretched. Bailey laid his head on the pillows beside
me. No fighting for rights tonight. We were home.
Amazing how one gets accustomed to changes.

I was dozing off when I felt Bailey lift his head
in alarm. A car door slammed. How do dogs do
that? We both cowered on the bed as footsteps
sounded on the stairs to the third floor of my house.
It's the only way to get to the top floor. Isolated as
I am in this Mecca of surrounding medical buildings, every little sound carries like trumpets
blowing. We heard a key in the lock upstairs. The
thump of something heavy dropping to the floor.
Even a curse as the unknown person stumbled
against something. I grinned in the dark. I had rearranged the furniture upstairs.

Bailey must have felt the tension leaving me; the
fur on his neck unruffled, but he still turned to me
for reassurance.

"It's okay, sweetie. It's just Steven Hyatt." He
was the only other person who had a key to the
upstairs. "He'll keep till morning. Go to sleep
now."

And he did, snoring softly in my ear as I lay
awake, exhausted but trying to figure out what tomorrow would bring.

Twenty-Two

"Good morning, Steven," I said to Steven Hyatt the next morning, when he showed up at the back door as I was making coffee. I had decided to pretend that his appearance was an everyday occurrence, not that he had landed with a thump in the middle of the night.

"Good morning to you, Honey," he replied. He is so quick to catch up on my games.

Remembering this and all the games of our childhood made me smile, and I broke the pretense and threw my arms around him. "Oh, you goose. You scared us to death last night. What on earth are you doing here?'' I hugged his neck, and he smelled like warm sleep and worn travel.

Steven was holding one hand behind him but brought it around to complete the hug he was giving me. "I came to bring you this," he said.

I studied the box carefully. "It's a computer game. You flew in from New York to bring me a computer game?''

"No, I brought you ten computer games."

I was flabbergasted. "Well, thank you very much. But did you ever hear of UPS?''

In mock despair he exclaimed, "What? Trust my favorite, tried-and-true games to a shipping clerk? I don't think so.''

He poured himself a cup of coffee as I went through the plastic garbage sack I now saw at his feet.

"These are your games? Your very own?'' I could now see that the boxes had been opened. I scanned the titles at the top of the bag. Caesar's II, Kyrandia, Lords of the Realm I and II, Heroes of Might and Magic. "Excuse me, you won't send them UPS and yet you bring them in a torn garbage bag? May I ask why?''

"I wanted to give you something, and since you have all the money in the world to buy whatever you want, I wanted to give you something personal.''

"Conquest of the New World is personal?'' I asked as I pulled another box out of the tattered plastic.

He feigned being hurt. "Of course it is. I spent hours building those towns, conquering those enemies. My heart and soul are in those CD-ROMs. They are the most valuable and sacred things I own.''

"Okay. Thank you,'' I said again. "But that doesn't explain why you felt you had to give me something,'' I corrected. *"Bring* me something personal in person.''

"Well, I don't have a dog." He grinned.

The dog in question took this opportunity to jump high on Steven's chest, overjoyed to see a same-sex person in the house. Steven put down Deadlock, A Planetary Conquest, to wrestle with Bailey. I smiled to watch them do their guy thing on my kitchen floor.

Despite its being the middle of July, Steven had a pale Yankee complexion that I could now see could be attributed to hours of unending computer play. Bailey knocked his wire-rimmed glasses sideways in his enthusiasm to lick the face of his new friend. Steven just sat in the middle of the floor while Bailey washed his face with kisses but yelped when the dog started morning ablutions on his frizzy brown and blond hair. When Steven ducked to escape the dog's tongue, I could see the beginnings of an early bald spot at the top of his head. My heart swelled as I looked at this endearing imperfection.

I read somewhere sometime that when a mother looks at a baby, her eyes respond to the love by changing size and that when a woman or a man saw the person they loved, their heart swelled and they felt it in the middle of their chest. This is what I felt when I watched Steven Hyatt, wan and vulnerable, on my kitchen floor. I never had experienced this feeling before. Guess I really did love Steven.

"You don't have a dog? What does that mean?"

"Harry gave you a dog. That's pretty personal in my book. Like giving you a child. I just came down to check out the temperature."

"Like a big brother checking to see what his intentions are?"

"Not exactly, but close." He smiled.

I took Bailey outside and clipped his collar to the extra-long chain I have staked in my yard. When the clinic next door did their landscaping, they had included my postage stamp yard in their plans, giving me both a gazebo and a small garden, but their plans had included tearing down the surrounding fence. Bailey immediately strained the chain to the limit, eager as always to dig up my iris bed. The chain fell short by one foot, but he always tried the limit every morning when I put him out.

I had a reply formulated by the time I returned to the house.

"You *know* Harry had an emergency in London. You can't take a pet into England without a six-month quarantine. I'm sure he will be back soon. That's all there is to it."

"Have you heard from him?" Steven was now sitting at my picnic bench kitchen table, sipping his coffee and adding way too much sugar to it.

I paused while pouring my own cup.

"No, and I'm a little worried about that. What if his mother died?"

Steven's eyes danced over the top of his cup as he lifted it. "What if his mother isn't his mother?"

"Come again?"

"I got to thinking about the note you read to me on the phone. The one Harry sent you by taxi. When he said 'Mother is ill,' that could have meant Mother the country, not Mother my mom. He *is* retired CIA."

"Secret Service, they call it in Great Britain, Steven. Remember James Bond?"

"Yes, well, whatever." His eyes gleamed.

"I've got it. I've got it," came a scream as Janie bounded down the stairs two at a time. Not bad for an older woman. She ran just as bouncy into the kitchen where Steven Hyatt's presence stopped her cold.

"Steven."

"Janie."

Neither had known the other was here. I'm not good at small talk.

I am good at breakfast, though. The only meal at which I somewhat excel. But the two plotters in my house didn't even notice the strawberry print paper napkins or perfectly poached eggs on their Eggs Benedict muffins with homemade hollandaise sauce. *Just a little something I whipped up,* I said to myself as they wolfed it down.

"So, see," Steven explained to Janie, *"Mother* is a euphemism for England. They have called him back into service for a special secret project."

"Well, it came to me that what Clover meant by being an author is that *she* wrote *For All the Wrong Reasons,*" Janie told Steven.

"Reckon that will put off his wedding plans for Honey anytime soon. Bet he's not even in London at all." Steven was weaving his own web.

"So when Twyman found out that Clover was

writing her memoirs, he came to beg her not to tell the world he was a phony.'' Janie matched his declarations tit for tat.

"That's why he brought her the ring,'' Janie said as she topped him.

But not for long. "Bet Harry's in a foreign prison right now,'' Steven wished.

"He is?'' Steven finally got her attention.

"She did?'' Janie's words about Clover's writings sank in.

I ate my absolutely perfect poached egg in silence. When you can't compete . . .

Twenty-Three

By the time Silas dropped by unexpectedly with donuts, I was out of the egg-cooking mood so I hid the signs of the special sauce and joined him for a little dunking.

Janie and Steven were in the kitchen, washing the dishes. Okay, Janie was washing the dishes; Steven was hovering over her, telling her what he thought Harry was up to.

"Didn't know Hyatt was here," said Silas, drowning a cake donut.

"His sleigh landed last night. I don't know his plans. When he comes down to earth, maybe I can figure them out. What's up with you?''

Silas hunkered over his coffee cup, his big hands hiding the tea rose china. ''Sometimes I think you're out there, too. In space. But . . .'' he said in a concessional tone, ''this time you might be right. God, I hate to say that.''

''Of course, I'm right.''

Pause. Two beats.

''Okay, I'll bite. I'm right about what?''

''Your Towerie thing.''

I squealed. ''Ah ha! It was murder. I'm right. I'm right.'' There was a little singsong to my words.

''Whoa. I'm not saying murder. I'm saying it wasn't as all cut and dried as it appeared,'' Silas replied, not ready to give me the whole enchilada.

''What do you know? What do you know?'' I asked, sounding like a character from *Guys and Dolls*.

Silas was a big man in more ways than one. When he was right, he was firm. When he might be wrong, he was willing to look at new facts. Some call that waffling. I call it smart. ''You know how I admire you? How I think you're almost always on target?''

Well, no. I hadn't known that.

He had to go and ruin the compliment by over-explaining. Just like a man.

''Even when you're wrong, like you were accusing Bondesky of killing Steven Miller, I know you're on the right track to something." He took another donut, his third. "So I checked a little more on Towerie."

I handed him a fourth donut from the box. Like putting coins in a slot machine for the next turn. With enough coins or donuts, you win a prize. "And?" I encouraged.

"It seems that a blood sample is routinely drawn during an ambulance ride. The EMTs drew one on Towerie on the way to the hospital."

"Silas, he was dead."

"Nevertheless, they took a blood sample."

I guessed. "And they found poison, right?"

"No. No, that's not the point."

I handed him the last donut. "The point being . . . ?"

He looked into his empty coffee cup. I pushed my untouched cup over, and he dunked the thing. As it entered his mouth, he said something.

"What? I didn't catch that. The vial with Twyman's blood is where?"

"Missing," Janie said from the kitchen door.

"Stolen," Steven Hyatt declared, leaning around Janie to get his two cents' worth in.

How do they do that? All I had heard from Silas's crummy mouth was, *"Xde thar vireal gore."*

"Gone? The blood sample is missing? It was stolen?" I asked.

My perfect detective cleaned out his vocal chords with a gulp of coffee from my cup. "Right."

Janie sat down at the table, flipping open her notebook that she fished from her robe pocket. "It could have been a hospital error," she declared as she wrote down the information.

"They make lots of errors in hospitals," Steven agreed. "Look how many people wind up dead in hospitals."

"I'm pinning it on Clover," Janie said. "It goes with my theory."

Silas flipped open his notebook. "That theory being . . ."

Always glad to have center stage with Silas, my mystery buff friend began telling him about her verdict that Clover Medlock had killed her ex-husband. I could not believe that Silas was writing down her conclusions. I guess if you don't have much to go on, any straw in the wind is worth scribbling down.

I took the empty coffee cups and depleted donut box into the kitchen. Steven followed me. "You don't agree with Janie?"

"That Clover did it? I don't like to think so, Steven. I like Clover."

"You like Bondesky, too, but that didn't stop you

from claiming he killed Steven Miller,'' he reminded me.

"Maybe I learned something from that mistake,'' I argued. "That's what mistakes are for.'' I crushed the box and opened the pantry door to deposit it in the trash. There was a time when I wouldn't have opened the pantry door on a dare. Now I considered the gaily painted, brightly lit room under the stairs the source from which all blessings flow. That change only confirmed my conviction. "I'm more cautious in my accusations now.''

I returned to the dining room where Silas and Janie were ending their mutual note taking. "I have a question.''

"Yes?'' they both asked.

"Would Clover Medlock have had access to the vial? Would she have even known about it?'' I figured that would squelch the speculations.

Silas was ready for that one. "Actually, Clover Medlock has the key to the whole hospital, hypothetically speaking. She was the one who bailed them out of their last fund-raising event. They've named the new blood lab The Clover Medlock Laboratory. So, yes, I think she could have had access. And she did show up at the hospital to claim the body.''

"See?'' said Janie.

Twenty-Four

An advantage of one having money is giving oneself a holiday. In fact, three days.

Of course the Day-Timer in me made certain that all bases were covered. I assured Juliana I would indeed not only attend her Friday computer/inventory party but that I also would bring additional help. Then I informed Steven Hyatt and Janie of their Saturday plans.

And on an impulse, I called Kantor.

"So why would I want to come to a computer party? Remember, my Honey, computers are why I left the business."

"Yes, Kantor, I remember. But I wanted to show you what I'm doing now and I know you want to meet Juliana. Papyrus used to be one of your favorite stores and now that her aunt is dead, Juliana would benefit from your expertise. Please?" I begged.

We left it with an "I'll think about it."

Business in hand, I turned toward a hedonistic experience and Steven Hyatt and I had three days of a glorious orgy in my war room.

"Higher, Honey. Aim toward the center."

"Steven, he won't be still. Is he a wizard or a warrior?"

"There, you got him. Now pick up your prize."

"Ahhh, it's gold."

"My turn."

Steven was determined to load all ten of the games he had brought me and teach me the rudiments of each. We had worked out a polite ritual of changing places whenever it was the other's turn to play one of the games. I would play my turn and then get up and quietly move to the chair that he had been sitting in as he instructed and kibitzed through my play. Likewise, Steven would get up and bow when his turn was over and we sidestepped each other to claim our chairs.

Janie was fascinated. "Seems to me, it would be

easier to get two computers," she observed after one of our place-changing maneuvers.

"Oh, yes. Steven, let's go get another computer," I agreed.

"Next time, Honey. This will do for now, although it would help to have chairs on rollers."

"And you can get a LAN card and play side by side," said Ms. Potter, who had come to give me another lesson but stayed to play. "I want to be red this time. It's easier to see on the screen."

Who would have thought that our Ms. Potter was a secret game player?

"You'll stay for lunch, won't you, Evelyn?" asked Janie. She had not joined us for the game sessions; instead, she had turned my kitchen into a version of a local La Madeleine's. Steven and I reckoned that was how she was working through the separation which, so far, she had refused to discuss. She fixed enchiladas and homemade guacamole when Silas came to dinner and fresh chicken salad for Ms. Potter. Her meat loaf was out of this world, and her pies equal to the Blue Bonnet Bakery. I knew my kitchen had never seen the likes. Not even when Aunt Eddie was alive. Although it was said that Aunt Allie had been the cook.

Finally though, Steven had enough of home cooking and declared it a Texas ethnic night, and we all adjourned to Massey's for chicken-fried steak. Silas joined us, and we took one of the long church tables in the back room. I was famished.

It was a compliment to my hardworking window units that we had all forgotten about the Texas July heat. The one in the war room was newly installed, and I quickly shucked the sweatshirt I had donned to fight dragons on the monitor. Janie hadn't complained, so I guess the one in the dining room was still cooling the downstairs, even through her cooking frenzy.

On the way to Massey's I told my van load of passengers about the "swamp" fans that were still in operation when I was born. "You would go out every hour or so, depending on the heat, and water down the straw pads around the unit. The pump was supposed to circulate water, but it was just so hot that the water would evaporate before it could make it to the top of the straw. Father and I would go out together, and he would always turn the hose on me, and Mother would always fuss," I recalled with some nostalgia.

"Oh, right. I remember those units. Evaporative coolers were what they were called, Honey," said Janie with Ms. Potter agreeing with her.

"They kept the downstairs fairly cool if a bit damp. I guess those two window units, the one in my bedroom and the dining room, were the first things I bought on my own after my parents died."

"Little by little, you're changing the house," said Steven. "Making it your own."

"You think?" I asked as I slid into a parking place at Massey's. "Do you think I'm changing, too, Steven?"

"When you let me wipe you out in Heroes, then I will think you've changed."

"Don't sulk," I told him as we locked the van against the still shimmering heat. "You know I can't stand it if you attack me. That's why I only like those games where we can play partners."

He protested. "But that way, some of the games never end."

"I know, but we kill all the bad guys like green and gold and purple, but we stay friends forever. That's the way I like to play."

"So I'm finding out," he muttered.

"Playing games is hard work," I declared between bites of my order.

Again, to my surprise, Ms. Potter was packing away her share of gravy and biscuits. "Well, I don't often indulge in either games or such rich food. I mostly eat fruit and salads."

"That accounts for your outstanding figure, Ms. Potter," said Steven graciously.

"And exercise. I walk four miles every day," she added.

"If Honey keeps on playing games and eating like a horse, she would do well to follow your example, ma'am."

I kicked him.

"Hey, this is a holiday. Anything goes," I defended. "We all go back to work on Saturday, you know. 'Cept you, Silas. And, Ms. Potter, I can't thank you enough for joining us. We'll have Papyrus whipped in no time."

"I'm still not sure what my role in all this work is going to be," said Steven.

"Comic relief?" I suggested and received a kick in return.

"Hey, we should ask Bondesky to join us, too. Bet he could help Juliana with her books." My suggestion sounded good to me.

"He's busy Saturday," announced Ms. Potter. Her attack on the chocolate pie told me that she was not pleased with Bondesky's weekend plans.

"Doing what?" I pursued.

"I believe he has an engagement with one of your friends," she replied, taking a very unladylike bite of pie.

"Clover?" I guessed.

"I couldn't say," she said as she turned the fork into a weapon against the pie.

"Clover Medlock?" Silas picked up on the conversation. "I talked to her again yesterday."

"What did she say?" Janie asked. "Did she know anything about the missing blood samples?"

"I couldn't say," he responded.

I still refused to believe Clover could have had something to do with Twyman's death. "You know," I mused out loud, "there *were* three other wives who were not too friendly with Twyman."

"Well, I've only met Gabriella, and she gets my vote," said Steven. "Wow, what a witch."

"But she wasn't here, and Clover was," said Janie.

"Wonder what Babe and Marcie are like," I said.

Steven and Janie exchanged a knowing glance.

"What?" I asked.

"Nothing," said Steven. Then knowing I wouldn't let it go, he added, "Okay, let's put it this way. I'm going to your grand computer party in Jacksboro on Saturday; then you have to do something for me in return."

"What?" Suspicious this time.

Steven smiled that I-hate-it-when-you-smile-at-me-that-way smile and Janie giggled.

Uh-oh, I thought.

Twenty-Five

Saturday was just as hot as the preceding days had been, and we used up the cool air flowing from the weak unit at Papyrus by ten in the morning. But we were having too much fun to notice.

Divine providence had surely sent Ms. Potter to us. That woman could enter ISBN numbers into the new computer quicker than we could spout them off. The system we finally worked out was that we would gather ten books each and stand in line for her to enter them as we called out the title, author, and ISBN. Then we would reshelve the books, marking them with a Post-it or gummy dot to show that the book was successfully entered in the system.

Janie helped keep track of which area was next in the surprisingly well-stocked bookstore. Juliana and three of her yuppie-in-training friends kept the line moving as they good-naturedly followed Janie's orders. Steven's job was to keep Kantor happy and Bailey entertained. I did everything else, but my main job seemed to keep everyone well watered with cold bottles of Evian.

Kantor had shown up with reluctant eagerness and had been welcomed with a hug from Juliana, who had known of him from her aunt, and squeals from Janie. Kantor had been her regular book rep at Pages before I took the route. After throwing up his hands at the computer system, the old man had kept us in stitches, telling stories about some of the authors we would call out to Ms. Potter.

Kantor knew Bailey, too, from his time on South Padre, back during the days when he helped Harry get started with Sandscript.

"He seems to remember me," Kantor said as Bailey danced around him with happy yips.

"Seems so," I agreed. I had decided to bring Bailey with us, putting his crate in the van to house him if the day proved too much. I just didn't feel I could impose on Clover again.

"Where did you say Harry was?" asked Kantor.

"In an enemy prison," answered Steven.

"Undercover," said the irrepressible sleuth Janie.

"With his sick mother," I insisted.

Kantor looked confused but just smiled and nodded at all three of our versions on the whereabouts of the missing Harry.

"How are we doing?" I asked Ms. Potter. "Is the system going to work?"

"Good enough for government work," she answered. I was really beginning to like Ms. Potter.

We had had breakfast at the Green Frog, so Kantor and Steven made a run to Herd's for hamburgers when we took a break for lunch. It was the first time I had really gotten to speak to Juliana's friends, Molly, Robin, and Marsha, whom everyone called Sasha.

Like Juliana, they were all my age, but oh, lord, what worlds apart our lives were.

As they sipped fresh bottles of Evian, they talked about foreign things like children and car pools and fitness classes. I tried to imagine me in their place and nearly freaked. The closest I had been to a child was my limited experience with Bailey, and I didn't think that would count with these sophisticated, professional mothers. When we had been inventorying the childcare section of the bookstore, they had all been familiar with the books. I knew more than I wanted to about child rearing when we finished the section.

Still I was curious about their lives. So I listened and learned. It was like being in Marriage class 101.

When Steven and Kantor returned with lunch, I whispered in his ear, "Is this the kind of life you foresaw for me when you said I should get married and settle down?"

He smiled his Hollywood/New York show biz grin and passed the burgers to the ladies. He didn't answer me, but the Bailey-like stupid adoration gaze he gave the barely perspiring tanned lovelies told me volumes.

I mopped my red, wet curls out of my face, ignored him, and turned to listen to Janie and Kantor.

Ms. Potter was also interested in their conversation, which I soon discovered revolved around Clover Medlock.

"Then you agree?" I heard her saying. "Clover Medlock *did* write *For All the Wrong Reasons*?"

"Remember, I knew Twyman Towerie well," replied Kantor. "I remember his journalist endeavors. The man didn't have an ounce of talent in him. So, yes, I always thought she was the author."

The conversation even interested Steven the Lothario.

"Then what about *Down by the Riverside*? If

Twyman didn't write well, how do you account for that book?" he asked.

Janie remembered. "Steven, you did say Gabriella Rusi was frightened about something when you mentioned *Riverside*?"

"Hmmm, not frightened, exactly. Startled maybe. Definitely uncomfortable with my asking about it," he said. "But believe me, I know Gabriella Rusi. She is a fantastic publicist, but I don't think she has an ounce of imagination in her. She couldn't have written that book."

"Well," contended Kantor. "I'm willing to bet that neither did Twyman Towerie."

Janie wondered, "If he didn't write *Reasons* or *Riverside*, what about *Casa Rojo*?"

"Ooooh," squealed Robin. "I loved that book. It's my favorite Twyman Towerie book. So different than the others."

"But just as brilliant," said Steven, rewarding Robin with a spare package of potato chips for her dazzling insight into literature.

"Better students of writing than we are have asked just these questions," said Kantor. "How did the man write three so different and yet intelligent and sensitive books? They called him a genius. I call him a fraud."

"Okay, he wrote *Reasons* while he was married

to Clover, *Riverside* while he was married to Gabriella, and *Rojo* while he was married to Marcie, right?'' I was trying to sort it all out.

''No,'' said Janie and Kantor.

''Twyman didn't write anything while he was married to Marcie. He was sick, remember, and she saved him.''

''He was married to that movie star—what's her name?—when he wrote *Rojo*,'' added Kantor.

''Babe,'' said Steven.

Leave it to him to know.

Twenty-Six

The first time one flies it should be a well-planned event. Insurance paid up and last will and testament made. That was exactly how I had planned my first flight earlier in the spring—a business trip to Boston—that was canceled when Steven Miller died in my living room. Maybe I would have actually boarded the plane. I will never know.

One's first flight should not be conceived in conspiracies and lies, although it would make a good movie title. One should not be coerced to drive one's best friend to the airport, forced to park in long-term parking, and led aboard a fun flight to Las Vegas.

Steven Hyatt thought it was so funny that he giggled. I do not like men who giggle.

In fact, as he strapped me in my seat, having arm-wrestled me down the aisle of the plane, I found I did not like Steven Hyatt at all.

"And Janie is in on this?" I asked.

"Yes. Yes. She packed your bag. That's why I *borrowed* your suitcase," he said as he did the thing I hated again.

God, I hated hating Janie, too.

"Bailey," I said weakly, looking for a last line of defense.

"It's perfect, if you stop to think about it. Janie is there to watch him."

"He'll miss me."

"Excuse me? Who do you think took care of Bailey while we played our marathon games? He adores her."

Defending my motherly instincts—which we both knew was a crock—got me off the ground at D/FW. A quick emergency Bloody Mary from a smiling waitress—oops, stewardess—got the plane into the air. "I have taken care of that dog beautifully. All his meals are on time and he only eats pizza on the weekends. I have not yelled at him for chewing sofa pillows and walk him every evening when the sun goes down. He sleeps in my bed and never goes thirsty. *What is that noise?''*

"It's only the wheels retracting into the plane. Now you will hear a slam as the wheel doors shut. Trust me, Honey, I know all the sounds a plane makes, and this one is doing nicely.''

"This is assurance from a man who doesn't know how to shave?'' Steven's lower jaw was patched with toilet paper from two cuts from his morning's ablutions.

"I used your razor. We'll pick up a new one in Vegas. They have razors in Vegas. *And* toothpaste, toothbrushes, and deodorant. This is not a foreign country.''

"Tell me again why we are going to Las Vegas.'' The Bloody Mary was kicking in. I was almost up to looking out the window.

"To meet Babe,'' Steven said again.

"You're sure she's there?''

"Yes, appearing at the MGM Grand. She's a headliner in one of the rooms. Just for another week,'' he added.

"Well, if I didn't hate you, I would say it was a good plan. But, since I do . . .''

"Relax, have another drink. This is not a long flight. You should have seen what I went through to get to Australia."

Flying is not so bad. I could get used to it. In fact, I think a hot-air balloon is more my speed. As we skimmed over the countryside, I was amazed at how much there was. How symmetrical the farmland was laid out and how the endless brown desert stretched in all directions, its surface cracked in the summer's heat. I imagined gliding over the mountains with their melting white caps in a gaily colored balloon. I could do this.

"You're almost forgiven," I told Steven as the plane began its descent into Las Vegas. "But I'm not sure about Janie."

"She's fine."

"I don't think she should be left alone at this time," I said, emphasizing *at this time*.

"Janie needs some time alone," he replied.

"She hasn't spoken about the separation at all," I countered.

"Well, not to *you*."

"To *you?*"

"Women have been known to confide in me, yes."

"Bull honk. But that's beside the point. What did she say?"

Next to a man giggling, I hate a man being smug.

"She's afraid she will disappoint you."

"Me?"

"Yes, and don't worry. Those are the wheels opening. This has been a smooth flight. You can let go of my arm now."

I turned from the sight of Las Vegas ascending— it seemed that way to me—and stared at Steven. "Why me? Why should I be disappointed in her?"

"Swallow hard and clear your head this way," he said as he held his nose and blew into his fingers. Yuck.

"My ears aren't stopped up."

"Yes, they are. You're shouting."

I did the nose and finger thing, but I used a Kleenex. He was right. The plane sounds came in too loud and too clear.

Steven went on talking, I'm sure to keep me occupied as we dropped lower and lower, the plane looking for a place to plop itself. "It's hard for a woman to walk away from a long relationship. Janie knew for years that her marriage wasn't working out. She doesn't hate her husband. Just wants out of a dead-end relationship. And she's afraid that you will turn sour on marriage, knowing hers didn't work out. It took lots of guts for her to walk away," he said admiringly.

"I'm sour on marriage, all right, but it has nothing to do with Janie."

"I don't understand," he said as the plane found its resting place. "Why? Your parents had such a good one."

I have never seen ground go by so fast. I turned away from the window and tried to answer Steven. "Maybe that's it. Theirs was perfect. That's a hard act to follow. Mother and Father were totally devoted to each other. I don't know if I can give that much of myself up."

"They loved each other. That's got to count. And they had you."

"Yeah, that scares me, too," I confessed. "Kids. What do I know about kids? I can't even take care of a dog. I can take care of myself. That's about it."

Steven rented a red convertible, and we drove in from the airport with the top down. Twilight was just beginning to fade, and the unbelievable lights of Las Vegas slapped us in the face as we drove down the strip. There was excitement in the flashing neon that surpassed anything I had ever experienced. The people, the lights, and the commotion were overwhelming.

I was speechless.

Steven was wrong.

Las Vegas *is* a foreign country.

Twenty-Seven

Sometimes it pays to know the magic words.

In Vegas the words were, "Babe, could I bother you for a minute of your time? My name is Honey Huckleberry from Fort Worth, Texas. And, yes, I am a fan of your work, but what I want to see you about is that I was with your ex-husband when he died. Thought you might like to hear about his death."

Only one lie. I was not a fan of Babe's work. Was not even sure what it was she did except make the cover of *People* magazine once a quarter. And most of those mentions featured low cleavage evening gowns shot of Babe arriving or departing at those perpetual Hollywood events that *People* covered so religiously for those of us who considered a trip to the local Tom Thumb grocery an outing.

Steven was not surprised when the waiter brought our reply so quickly. It was scribbled on the bottom of my note to her. "After the show. In my dressing room. Babe."

We—or rather Steven—had made purchasing tickets for Babe's performance one of the first priorities of our visit.

My first priority was to see how much money I could lose before I hit the elevator to my room.

"I should have known better than to bring a game addict to Las Vegas," muttered Steven as he left the concierge's desk at the Flamingo. He took me by the elbow and trotted me toward the elevators.

"Did you see the cute slot machine with all the fireworks?" I asked. "Or the one with the cherries?"

"They *all* have cherries."

"Maybe, but this one had *double* cherries."

"May I suggest the nickel slots?"

"What? When they have five-dollar ones? Just think how fast your money would multiply."

"Divide," he corrected.

Our rooms were on the sixth floor and overlooked

the penguin pond. To the left of the black and white creatures slip-sliding in their pool like a crash scene of police cars in a movie were the actual flamingos.

"Oh, my, Steven. Just look at this. They're alive."

"You really do need to get out more, Honey," he said as he peered out the wall-sized glass window. "If you're into animals, we could go over to the Mirage and look at their registration desk. Now that's a sight."

"They have animals at the registration desk?"

"I'm not going to touch that one." He laughed. "I meant the mile-long fish tank behind the desk. I've spent hours there. There is this one fish that chases the others. He's about two feet round and is the bully of the tank."

"What kind?"

"I don't know. A fish is a fish to me."

He went on to his room, and I took the time to see what Janie had packed for me. I had gone to the airport in shorts and a T-shirt, which, from what I had seen from the airport and hotel lobby, was okay for Vegas.

There were a few new items in my wardrobe, I noticed.

I called Janie.

"What on earth is that fluffy nightgown thing you

packed? And that sweet white dress? And where is my old sleep shirt? And thanks for putting in all that money. I think I'm gonna need it here. They have all these games to play.''

"Oh, I wish I were with you."

"Come on out. Catch the next plane."

"Oh, you sweetie, I can't do that. I have Bailey and the house to watch."

That kind of worried me. "You're not afraid to be in the house alone? I mean, I'm not, certainly, but this is your first time. And, well, after Steven Miller died in my living room, I'm not certain the neighborhood is as safe as I would like to think it is."

She reassured me. "I'm perfectly happy here. We'll go to Vegas together another time. I wouldn't want to crash your honeymoon."

"Excuse me?"

"That's what the white dress is for. Is it okay for the wedding? I know it's simple and all, but I thought it was sweet. Looked like you."

I eyed the white eyelet sundress, its existence suddenly sticking out like a sore thumb in my closet. I repeated, "Excuse me? Who is getting married?"

Janie made a blissful noise into the telephone. "Well, he didn't actually say, but why else would Steven make all those wonderful romantic secret plans? I felt honored to be a part of them," she added humbly.

"Are you sure you're not a romance book aficionado, not a mystery book guru?"

"What do you mean? I think you and Steven make a cute couple."

What Steven had told me on the plane about Janie worrying about discouraging me from marriage made me bite my tongue. In a calm, very rational voice, I said, "Janie, dear, you know that if I get married, it will probably be to Harry. Steven Hyatt and I are just best friends, remember?"

"Harry is in prison for life," she announced.

In my very controlled voice that was cracking at the edges, I replied, "No, Janie. Steven Hyatt made that up. Harry will be home soon."

"Have you heard from him?"

"No, but I have faith."

"See, he's in the slammer in some foreign country. Probably Libya or maybe even Iraq."

"Janie," I screamed, "stop it."

After a pause, she timidly asked, "You really going to marry Harry?"

I looked out at the penguins doing their version of the crash scene in the *French Connection* and thought. Finally, I said, "You know, I don't think so."

"Honey, do you remember when I talked to Steven Hyatt on the phone and you asked me what he said and I didn't tell you?"

"Yeah."

"Well, he said he loved you. Really and truly loved you. And wanted to marry you. That he had always loved you. That's why it was no surprise to me that he showed up here. And I know you love him," she prattled on.

"Janie, you must have misunderstood him. Steven and I have never even exchanged a kiss— other than hello and good-bye ones. Geesh, we're beginning to sound like last Thursday's episode of *The Young and the Restless.*"

"I am not mistaken," she insisted. "That's why you are in Las Vegas."

"We are in Las Vegas to interview Babe about Twyman's death. I mean his life. Whatever. We're investigating something that the police seem to think is nothing."

"Yes, and when you two get married in one of those chapels, you'll be a married investigative duo—just like the Norths or Nick and Nora. Maybe Peter and Harriet?"

"Janie, that's it. I'm hanging up now. Leaving. Good-bye."

"Wait, Honey. I have one more question."

"What? What?"

"Can I borrow some money from the piano bank?"

"Oh, lord, yes," I said contritely. "Janie, I'm sorry, I meant to tell you to take what you needed. I left plenty in there to run the house. In fact, I could run the White House. How much do you need?"

"Ten thousand."

Twenty-Eight

Anyone who knows me, really knows me, understands what a gentle person I am. I inherited the trait from my father, a dear, sweet soul who wouldn't hurt a fly. I have always been suspicious of my mother, however; even with her frail, wan ways, she had nerves of steel and what one *look* from her eyes could do to a noisy adolescent is legend.

That look was the one I gave Steven Hyatt the morning we met for breakfast at Lindy's in the Flamingo. I had lost forty-five dollars from the elevator to the open-air restaurant.

"What do you mean, I get to play the bad guy?"

"It's a cop's trick, Honey. When they interview someone, there's a good cop and a bad cop. The bad one hits the suspect with hardball questions that scare the suspect to death. The good guy is there to pick up the pieces, smooth the edges. That way he gets the trust of the suspect and can learn more. Don't look at me that way."

"Okay, one more time. Tell me again why it is that I get to have the heavy part?"

Steven cemented his toasted bagel with cream cheese and yawned as he said, "Because you're not. Bad, that is. It's reverse psychology. She will be expecting me—as the guy—to be the threatening one. We'll throw her offtrack," he ended confidently.

"Why do I think this isn't going to work?"

"Trust me. By the way, we don't meet Babe till tonight. What are your plans for the day?"

Okay, so I waited till he had a mouth full of goo. "First I thought we'd get married; then I'd like to win back some of the money I've lost already, and then . . . Steven? Are you okay? Here, drink some water."

"Get married? To whom?" he finally managed to squeak out the words.

"Why to *youm*. Isn't that the plan? According to Janie, this Vegas trip is where you propose. I thought over dinner and candlelight, but, hey, orange juice and bagels is fine with me. Was this to be a morning wedding or an afternoon affair?''

"Damn Janie."

"I don't think so. She has your best interests at heart. You've got to see this negligee set she put in my suitcase. Her idea of a bridal gown."

He wiped his mouth with the linen napkin. "You know Janie. She asks one question and hears only the answer she wants to hear."

"Yes, like we're madly in love and going to be the next Nancy Drew and Ned Nickerson. Only instead of living out of our roadster, we're gonna take the penthouse here at the Flamingo and swim in champagne while we experience true love."

"You're being tacky."

"Ah ha. . . . I'm just practicing my bad-guy routine."

"Yeah? Well, it's effective. So what questions do you plan on asking Babe?''

I whipped out my Day-Timer. I never leave home without it. "Suspect changes direction of conversation," I wrote as I said the words out loud.

"Okay. Okay. So Janie thinks you're in love with me instead of Harry."

"Me? In love with you? Nah, you've got it wrong. You're in love with *me*. You planned this whole Vegas gig so that we could get married in the chapel here.'' Both our gazes snapped to the penguins on parade outside of Lindy's and the nearby sign giving directions to the wedding chapel.

"Janie told you that? Wow, that's about what she told me about you. We've been set up, Honey, dear.''

"Then you don't love me?'' I asked.

"Of course I do. Now tell me those questions.''

"Okay. I love you, too. I think.'' I checked my notes. "First I'm going to offer my condolences.''

"Nope, won't work. I get to do that. I'm the good guy.''

"Oh, right. Well, then I'll just go right into the hard stuff. Like, when did you first notice that Twyman was a liar and a word thief? I think that should start things off nicely, don't you?''

"What's your follow-up?'' he asked.

"Babe, did you kill Twyman? And, if not, do you know who did?''

"Works for me. Wanna go gamble now?''

"Sure.''

I fell in love with the lights, bells, and whistles that was casino music. I loved the whirring of the slots, the clink of the coins, and the occasional shouts of winners and losers. I found this one machine with double cherries, right behind the give-

away car, and you could sit there for hours and nice
ladies brought you Cokes and coffee. And you
didn't even have to get up to make change. The
machine made it right there for you every time you
slipped in a twenty or a fifty. Although, it spit out
the fifties a lot, obviously as suspicious as I about
the new Franklin look.

After a while—hours?—Steven came up behind
me and sat down at the Double Diamond beside me.
"So, are you ahead or behind?"

"Don't ask. Wasn't it great of Janie to put in so
much money for me?"

"Right. Super of her, considering it was your
money. Do you have any left?"

"Well, I'm only playing quarters now, but when
I run out, I go over there to that dollar slot and win
it back."

"Excuse me, you're winning at the dollar slots
and losing here? Why aren't you playing the dollar
slots all the time?"

"I like this machine. It knows me."

He idly put a quarter in the Double Diamond and
hit triple Double Diamonds resulting in revolving
lights and colored bells. Or some such. I was too
frustrated to think clearly.

"How? Why?"

Steven accepted a complimentary scotch from the

cutely dressed lady with the tray as another attendant took down the information he needed from
such a big winner. Steven pocketed the dough and
stretched. "Think I've had about enough of this. I'm
starved. Wanna eat Chinese?"

"No, thought I would start with a Caucasian," I
said. "I have one in mind."

"Honey, honey. You can't get upset over this
stuff. It's just another game. But actually, it's good
practice for you."

"How so?"

"Think how mean you're gonna feel tonight
when you meet Babe."

"Right. I planned it so it would work out that
way. Okay, let's go meet your Chinese," I said as
I slid off my seat.

"One more thing I've been thinking about
though," Steven said as we wound our way through
the casino floor.

"Yeah?"

"I want to know more about this negligee."

Twenty-Nine

When Steven and I showed our tickets at the door of Babe's late show, a strange-looking man stepped forward. He reminded me of a hawk: tall, thin, and gaunt; a scavenger hawk.

"Ms. Huckleberry?"

Startled, I said nothing, so Steven answered for me. "Yes, can we help you?"

He smiled at that. An inward smile at some private joke. "No, but I can help you."

I found my voice. "Excuse me?"

"Never mind. Babe sent me to find you. She's reserved some seats for you."

"Oh, well, please thank her then."

We followed the man, who didn't identify himself, winding our way through the tables to the front row. On the table in the center was a yellow reserved sign, for special guests, it read. Our guide whisked the sign away and made a low bow over the table. No one rushed to stop us, so Steven and I slid into the seats. The man smiled his ambiguous smile again, did a little bow, and disappeared.

"What was that all about?" Steven asked.

"I have no idea. Do you think this is for us?" I asked, indicating the floor caddy beside our table, filled with ice and champagne.

The question was answered by a uniformed waiter who appeared from nowhere and proceeded to open the bottle and pour us cold glasses of very good champagne.

The special attention did not go unnoticed by those around us as they craned their necks and whispered to one another, trying to place our faces with their images of celebrities.

Their curiosity was only heightened when Babe appeared following a Comedy Store warm-up act that was genuinely funny. We were relaxed and laughing when the lights went dark following the comedian's introduction of the one and only Babe. As they came on again in a blaze, almost too dazzlingly white and blue, I closed my eyes, only to open them as Babe appeared in the display. The crystals on her dress reflected the startling stage lights, and she appeared almost ethereal. The audience rose as one to give her a resounding cheer. Us included.

As the applause dimmed, so did the spotlights, leaving the star in a bath of a soft glow as she acknowledged the homage and stood, arms spread downward and head bowed. She raised her head and looked directly at me.

The audience followed her gaze. They watched as she smiled and I smiled back a reply to a question I saw in her eyes, a question to which I didn't know the answer. I didn't even understand the question, but our contact seemed to please her.

I didn't know what to expect from her performance. Other than knowing that Babe was one of those ubiquitous celebrities whose name and figure appears everywhere, I had never had the experience of seeing her actually perform. I had seen her on *Letterman*, recognized his respect for her as they giggled and chatted through a segment of the show. But I never really understood what she did.

What she did was magic.

Not the kind of magic that was being performed throughout Las Vegas as we sat watching Babe's performance. No card tricks, no sawing in half, no disappearing jungle animals, but a magic that could only be attributed to a real entertainer giving the performance of her life.

I hadn't known she sang, but she wrung tears with her heartrending blues tune. I hadn't known she was funny, but in a saucy bit, she winked and drew blushes from my escort and roars from the audience as she used Steven as a foil for a naughty joke. She strutted her magnificent figure across the stage, her trademark full bosom a source of awe to even my eyes as it sparkled and glowed in the neck-high crystal dress. She dipped, she bowed, she glittered. She held the audience, this small part of the world, for a brief interlude; for a small dot in the space of time, she held us all in her hands.

And then it was over.

The house lights came on, shocking us all into gasps. Babe had been there, and then she was gone. Suddenly, the applause that everyone had neglected to give her while she had been before us was deafening. Calls and whistles begged her to come back, but only the single white light on the stage carried a whisper of what had just transpired. The people finally began to quiet down, realizing it was truly over. They began to filter out of the large room. Silently.

"What was that?" I asked Steven.

"That was the one and only Babe," answered a voice at my elbow. Our hawk stood there, that smile on his face again.

"Yes," I agreed.

"She's waiting for you."

Steven and I followed him through a mirror that was a door. It seemed appropriate.

Show business truly is all blue smoke and mirrors. As we edged through the cables and backdrops backstage, the glamour of the moment began to fade, but I was still awestruck when our escort opened the door with the large gold star on it. He gestured for us to enter.

Babe was reflected a thousand times in the huge mirrors that lined the walls. She was greedily smoking a cigarette, huddled in a fluffy pink robe on a nondescript chaise longue. Her discarded crystal beaded dress, reflected only in dimmed makeup lights, had lost its glitter, as had the star who had worn it.

I spoke first. "Miss Babe, that was a wonderful show."

She raised her head. "Yes? You liked it?"

"Liked it? It was the most fantastic show I've ever seen." I didn't mention it was the first I had ever seen.

"And you?" She looked at Steven.

"Yes, ma'am. I've never seen anything like it," he said.

"It was the best show you've ever done, Babe," said the man in an unexpectedly soft voice. "The very best."

"Ah, good. It is good to go out being the best," she whispered.

"Pardon?" I said.

The man answered my question. "She means this is her last show here at the Grand. We're closing tonight."

"I'm Honey Huckleberry," I said to him, hoping for a name. "And this is my friend, Steven Hyatt."

"Kevin Richardson," he said reluctantly.

Babe repeated my name. "Honey Huckleberry. What a name. You should be in show business, Honey. You're too young and pretty to be a sleuth. Do you sing?"

"No, ma'am, I don't. Not at all. But, what do you mean? A sleuth?"

She ignored my question and turned to look at Steven. "And how handsome you are. You look familiar to me. You *are* in show business, yes?"

"Yes, ma'am, I am. Well, I'm a movie director. Maybe you've seen one of my films?"

She murmured, "Hyatt. Hyatt. Yes, you did that little avant-garde film that received such interesting reviews. What are you doing now?"

Flattered that she recognized his name, Steven told her about his new film, due in theaters in a few weeks. How he had also written the screenplay, and that he had filmed most of it in Australia.

"I shall look forward to seeing it," she said graciously.

"Miss Babe, we don't want to take up much of your time," I said. "I just wanted to tell you about Twyman. Thought you might like to know about his death. And I have just a few questions."

Continuing to ignore my digression, Babe asked, "And are you two in love? You look like a bride, Honey. Kevin, I think they must be on their honeymoon, don't you?"

Kevin Richardson lit a cigarette and gave it to Babe. "Oh, definitely, Babe. They have that look."

"Well, we're not. On our honeymoon," I said. "I'm sorry to have disturbed you, Miss Babe. I just thought that maybe you could answer a few questions that have been bothering me. It was upsetting to be next to Mr. Towerie when he died." My voice trailed away.

Babe sighed. "Oh, all right. Clover did tell me

you were persistent. She crushed out her cigarette, lit another, and looked at me with a very tired face that the heavy stage makeup couldn't cover.

"Clover? You've talked to Clover Medlock about me?"

Thirty

Sixteen hours later, I sat at my own kitchen table, eating fresh tuna sandwiches that Janie had arranged attractively on a large glass plate and greedily drinking cold iced tea. The interview with Babe seemed like a dream. In fact, the whole Las Vegas interlude seemed incongruous with my small kitchen and the warm, yellow dog that snuggled close to my side. I gave Bailey a hug and part of my sandwich.

I reached for another one. "I ought to save one for Steven, I guess."

"There's plenty," Janie argued. "Eat. Eat. So you can tell me everything."

"It was strange. Not at all as I had imagined it would be," I told her.

"And you've got to know, Janie, Honey doesn't follow game plans," said Steven as he came in the back door. I had left him to bring in the luggage while I ran into the house, eager to see Janie and Bailey, eager to be with their energy and enthusiasm for life.

I protested. "Steven, how could anyone be a bad guy to that poor woman? Honestly, Janie, she was just worn out. I'm surprised she saw us at all."

Janie poured Steven a glass of fresh tea. "But did she answer any questions?"

"Oh, my, yes. What do you want to know? That she's retiring from show business? Or that she didn't love Twyman one little bit? That her scary friend Kevin actually wrote *Casa Rojo*?"

"Well, I'll be hornswoggled. She told you all that?"

"Right. And when I asked her why Twyman would have asked me about someone trying to kill him, she just said, 'Who wouldn't want to kill him?' "

Janie stood with her hands on her ample hips and shook her head in amazement. "Good lord, did she confess?"

"No," Steven answered for me as he reached for

a piece of chocolate cake, having eaten three of the sandwiches. "She just said it was time for everyone to know the real Twyman Towerie. That they had married because she had fallen for his fame and what she supposed was genius. Sort of like Marilyn and Arthur Miller. How she had introduced him to Kevin Richardson and encouraged him to read Kevin's manuscript."

I chimed in, "Yes, and how shocked they both were when *Casa Rojo* came out, and it had Twyman's name on it. That's when she left him."

"But she didn't tell?"

"No, and neither did Kevin. She didn't want her public to think her a fool. She has a certain image, you know."

"But I don't understand. Why didn't Kevin Richardson tell?"

"For the same reasons," Steven answered. "He didn't want scandal to touch Babe; they've been friends for ages, and he couldn't prove he had written the book. He's her sorta manager and no one knew he was writing. Twyman was the only one he had shown his work to."

"So why did she tell all of this to you two?"

"She told us that Clover had called her, told her about what Twyman had said to me before he died, and that I was asking a lot of questions. Babe said if the story was going to come out, she wanted it to be the truth," I told her.

Janie rolled her blue eyes heavenward. "What a tangled web we weave. . . ."

"Well, I'm weaving my next web in bed," announced Steven as he grabbed his bag and headed outside to go to his third-story room. "I'm exhausted."

"I'll bet you are tired, too, Honey," said Janie.

"Yes. No. I'm still too wound up, and I slept on the plane, believe it or not."

Janie sat down at the picnic bench kitchen table and took the last sandwich, much to Bailey's dismay. She looked down at the dog and said, "Don't even think about it. I made them, I'm eating it." To me she said, "Wait a minute. I thought all of Twyman's wives hated each other. Why was Clover calling Babe?"

"I have no earthly idea, Janie. Even with so many of our questions answered, there is still a lot we don't know."

"Like, if Clover wrote *For All the Wrong Reasons*, and Kevin Richardson wrote *Casa Rojo*, who wrote *Down by the Riverside*?"

"Right," I agreed. "And who actually killed Twyman?"

"You still think he was murdered?"

"Yes, I'm more sure of it than ever, but I can't go to Silas with just my hunches. We still have to prove it."

"Well, I know the perfect place to do it." Janie smiled as she spoke.

"Yeah? Where?"

She cut her bright blue eyes to the side. "You remember that ten thousand dollars I wanted from you?"

"Actually, yes. I've wondered why you needed the money. Not that you're not welcome to it," I added quickly.

Tears came to Janie's eyes. "Oh, Honey, I know that. I haven't said enough how grateful I am for your letting me stay here. I know how you feel about the house and having strangers in it."

"That was then, this is now, Janie. I seem to be getting used to people in the house. I'm growing up, and next year I'll be thirty and know everything. And"—I reached over and patted her arm—"you're no stranger. You're my best friend."

"Well, now I am officially your mother."

"Excuse me?"

"See, it's like this. You got several phone calls while you were gone. You remember Elaine Madison?"

"Yes, from the Arlington Friends of the Library."

"Right. She called early Saturday morning. Wanted to know how you were and so forth. I really like her. Anyway, we got to talking; she's still upset about Twyman dying at the luncheon, and she said something that surprised me."

"What?"

"Elaine said that she had known that Twyman was not well. When I asked what she meant, she said that was why his ex-wife Marcie had catered the lunch. I about fell over on the floor."

"No!"

"Yes, Elaine said that Marcie had called and volunteered to do the catering—for free—under the condition that no publicity was generated about it. Marcie said Twyman was ill and needed a special diet and she wanted to make sure he got it."

"But that's not true, Janie. Twyman had the same meal that I had. That you had. Baked chicken and mashed potatoes and lemon pie. Oh, and green beans," I added as I remembered one of them stuck up Twyman's nose.

"Ah ha . . . Did he? Elaine says not. She says his meal looked like everyone else's but was actually special stuff. Like fat-free potatoes and no sugar in the pie."

"Fooled me. Fooled him, too. You shoulda seen him dig into that pie. Hey, did he know that Marcie was catering?"

"No, Elaine said that was part of the condition. Marcie said that since the divorce and all, she had kept a watch on Twyman's health but that he resented it, so she did it surreptitiously."

"Janie, this is very serious. Does Silas know?"

She looked a little shamefaced. "Yes, he called, too, and I told him. He wants to see you. I lied— Silas is so easy to lie to—and told him you wouldn't be back till late tonight. I wanted to talk to you, and I knew you would need a nap. Oh, lord, I hated betraying Elaine, but, Honey, I agree with you, this is serious. So you can see why I did what I did."

"Does what you did have something to do with your being my mother now?"

Janie beamed. "See, Honey, how clever you are. Went straight to the heart of the matter. I just knew you would want to investigate this new turn . . ."

"Oh, right," I interrupted. "Janie, for the last time, I am not an investigator."

"You went to Vegas to see Babe."

"But I didn't *know* I was going to Vegas. I was shanghaied," I protested.

It was all the same in Janie's mind. "Nonetheless,

you did go and meet Babe. And you've met Clover.''

"That was because of the ring."

Janie raced on. "So, it made sense to me that you would want to meet Marcie. That's why I called The Bargello on Saturday."

"Marcie's spa?"

"Yes, that's why you need to take a nap. We're going to The Bargello for a week."

"Janie, even if we went to Jefferson to meet Marcie, it won't take a week; it's only a few hundred miles. And that's a *big* if."

I'm getting used to how Janie cuts her eyes around when she has an important announcement to make. "No, we're gonna be guests. Won't it be fun? I knew I couldn't use your name so I used mine."

"And said you were my mother," I added.

"Honey, that was the only spot that was open. Well, immediately. The Bargello mother and daughter week at the spa is next week. We leave in the morning. Early."

"And it costs ten thousand dollars?"

"Yes, isn't that amazing? Well, eight thousand with an extra thousand for Bailey and one for incidentals."

"We're taking Bailey?"

"Of course. What else would we do with him?

Steven told me he had to get back to Hollywood to do some publicity for the movie, and I don't really know any kennels here in Fort Worth. I just figured you would want him with you.''

"I didn't know Steven was leaving. And, Janie, what name did you use for me?"

"Why, your secret name, Honey. Lydia. You're Lydia Bridges for a week."

"And you're *Mom?*"

"Yes. I knew you'd understand."

Thirty-One

I slept so hard that Janie had to come and wake me up to tell me that Silas had arrived. It took me another twenty minutes to shower and slip on a clean pair of denim shorts and a T. Steven and Janie were sitting out back in the gazebo with Silas when I finally stumbled into the twilight of my backyard. Bailey was staked nearby, chewing on a rawhide bone.

Although I waved her down, Janie insisted on jumping up and getting me a fresh glass of iced tea. Steven followed her in the house with the tray, leaving me alone with Silas.

"I hear congratulations are in order?" he asked.
"For?"

"Why, you and Steven Hyatt. Janie's been filling
me in. Well, she was before Steven came down. I
always thought you and Steven were just buddies.
Guess I was wrong and I'm shit out of luck." He
grinned to show me there were no hard feelings.

I laughed. "Janie does have a motor mouth, it
seems," I said without denying or confirming.

The detective went on. "I always thought there
was something going on between you and that Brit
down in south Texas, the one I met when that guy
Jimmy was killed. Hey, I mean, you've got his dog,
after all."

Before I could fully explain about either Steven
or Harry, Silas continued, "Actually, its okay. You
were right about that Abbie Gardenia. See, I've
called her a few times; we've had some drinks, did
a flick. I kind of like her, you know. But, reckon
I'll always wonder whether you and I could have
hit it off."

Silent, I pondered on his backhanded compliment
as I watched Steve Hyatt return with a laden tray.
His frizzy hair stood on end from his nap, his long
legs were bowed and pale extending from his rum-
pled Australian khaki shorts, his skinny arms sup-
porting the tray looked inadequate for the job.

Squinting my eyes, I thought I could see the beginnings of a receding hairline above his crooked wire-framed glasses.

I watched as he handed first me and then Silas a frosty glass from the tray. For a brief second, he and Silas stood side by side. Silas's blond hair stirred in the warm breeze that signaled the first of the night's relief from the heat of the day. His sky blue eyes crinkled in a smile, and his square, solid jaw looked as strong as a bank vault. I looked him over slowly and appreciated the way his tanned muscles rippled with the movement all the way up the sleeves of his stylish pastel madras shirt, which was neatly stuffed into crisp, pleated chinos. Oh, my. They both turned to me and grinned, the detective raising his glass in salute. "Here's to you and Steven," he said.

For another brief second, I scanned my mind for all the options. Then I looked over at Steven's astounded hazel eyes. To my surprise, I just smiled and said, "Thank you, Silas."

Steven dropped the tray, of course, and in the confusion to clean up, Bailey gleefully snuffled over to eat the sandwiches Janie had made. I noticed that they were both cheese and tomato and potted meat sandwiches as they disappeared into Bailey's mouth. "Reckon y'all know what this means," I said.

I am learning to be so bad.

"Marriage?" asked Silas with a knowing grin on his face.

"Marriage?" croaked Steven with a caught-in-the-headlights look.

"Oh, you sillies," I answered in my best Southern belle imitation. *Eat your heart out, Scarlett,* I thought as I told the Tarleton twins, "I mean I reckon we'll just have to go out to eat. Y'all want barbecue?"

Over ribs, ranch beans, and potato salad at the Railhead, Silas once more expressed his concern about my so-called investigation of Twyman Towerie's death. With all the blabbing Janie had been doing, I wondered if she had clued him in to Babe's motives for killing her ex-husband. Still in my GWTW mood, I said sweetly, "Oh, you goose. You know I'm not an investigator. Why, I don't have an idea in the world about who would kill Mr. Towerie. I've forgotten all about that. Steven and I just went out to Las Vegas to get me over my fear of flying." I did clean up the act a little bit as I declared, "I don't know anything about murders and investigating."

Silas bought it, but Janie and Steven looked like I had lost my last marble. "You've got that right, Honey," he said as he hoisted his ice-encrusted beer glass. "I've talked to Lennox, and he says to forget

it all. Like I said from the first, it's over and done
with.''

"You tell them, Silas," agreed Steven. "And
while you're at it, tell them how stupid it is to be
going to meet Marcie."

"You're going to see Marcie?" asked Silas.

Janie jumped in with, "Oh, no, Silas. It's just
with that story on CBS about Twyman, they showed
some shots of The Bargello, and Honey and I got
to talking about how out of shape we are—and of
course, I'm a few pounds overweight. So we thought
what fun it would be to spend a week doing girl
stuff and getting back in shape and all. I'm sure we
won't even see Marcie Coleman."

Silas being Silas, he bought it. "Good. 'Cause
Lennox told me to tell you two to back off. He's
worried that y'all will do something dumb and get
in trouble." He laughed as he finished his beer.
"Reckon you can't get into trouble going to a carrot
farm, can they, Steven?"

Dubious, but loyal, Steven said, "Reckon not, Silas." It was a true macho moment as the men joked
about facials and massages. I pinched Janie's arm
hard as I watched her try to control her tongue. We
both sat there with barbecue sauce smiles pasted on
our faces.

Back at the house, as Silas drove off with a wave,

Steven turned to us. "I've just thought of something. This little trip to The Bargello, it wouldn't have anything to do with the fact that I told you that I saw on Gabriella's calendar that all the exes are meeting there on the eighth, would it?"

"Was that the date? I'd clean forgotten that," said Janie as she tripped up the front steps to the house.

"Right," called Steven after her. "Like hell you did." He turned to me, abandoned by my cohort. "And as for you, you've got some explaining to do. Although I think Silas is right; you won't be in any danger at The Bargello with all those fat women and celery stalks, I still think it's a dumb idea. Ah ha, not so fast, young lady, you've got another question to answer."

"Oh?" I stopped in my flight to join Janie. "And what would that be?"

"Are we getting married, or what?"

Thirty-Two

"Janie, tell me again when you became obsessive about murders and mysteries," I said to her as we sped along I-20 to Jefferson. I was trying to figure out why I was a passenger in my own Plymouth Voyager, sipping hot coffee through a plastic vent in the travel cup Janie had pressed into my hands as she steered me in the early morning cool before the sun dried out the day again.

"The very first mystery I read—well, the first one I remember registering—was John D. MacDonald's *The Deep Blue Good-Bye*. I had a broken leg, fell off my clog in the garden, but that's another story,

and someone brought me some books. *Blue* was one
of them. Back in seventy, I think. I followed Travis
McGee all through the rainbow of his mysteries after that. Then, you're right, I just became obsessed.
Went back and did Christie and then Chandler. Oh,
and James. The new ones, too.''

The steam gradually dissipated from my new sun-
glasses and I could actually gulp the caffeine stim-
ulant. I was getting out of shape. With my work
schedule shot, I didn't know whether I was coming
or going these days. ''But the idea that you can get
involved, solve mysteries? That came from reading
books?''

There had to be some reason we were headed for
a showdown with the ex-wives club.

''Yes, sorta. Mystery critics are such purists. I
don't know if Robert Ludlum is considered a mystery writer or not. There's protocol to a real mystery,
you know. You have to have a crime, an investigator, clues, and finally, retribution for the crime.
What I liked about Ludlum is that he always had an
innocent person who, by accident or coincidence,
became very much involved in villainy and was in
great danger before solving the murder, rape, or con-
spiracy.''

''I don't like the great danger part,'' I said.

She ignored me and went on, lost in her justifications. "So, yes, I always kinda fantasized about being the innocent one caught up in a major crime." She laughed as she cut her eyes toward me. "And solving it, of course."

"You may be right about this being a major crime, but not for the reason we think. It's not Twyman's death that is going to create headlines, unless we amateurs get lucky at The Bargello; it's his life. Listen to this." And I read her a letter I had received from Kantor, thanking me for including him in the Jacksboro workday at Papyrus. "He goes on to say he still has the same lowly opinion of computers, but all in all had a great day. What is really interesting is that he is still on the trail of who wrote Twyman's books. Says that's the real scandal. Wants to know more if we find anything out."

"See, puzzle pieces. That's what it's all about. Figure out one thing, and another piece of the puzzle fits. Then it leaves a gaping hole to be filled before the picture becomes clear. But you always have the clue of the interlocking pieces. What once was a flower becomes a stem, and you work your way through it all, right down to the roots."

God, I thought, *she is crazy.* I'm on the road to an asylum with an escaped inmate. Had I gone willingly? Would I read it that way in the headlines? Would I still be alive to read? Janie's fantasies were of daring deeds and stupendous adventure. Mine were more like images of the waiting grave plot next to my parents at Rosehill. I was between them, of course.

Janie disturbed this soulful image by asking, "Okay, it's your turn, Honey. Why are you going along with this?"

Why indeed?

I fit the protocol requirements. Innocent bystander. Caught up in a mystery by the sudden death of stranger. A diamond ring thrown in for good measure. Abundant clues and no danger yet, but who knew what we would find in the swirling waters of a Jacuzzi? And I had a sudden chill when I thought of the final condition of a real mystery: retribution.

I shuddered and said to Janie, "I have no earthly idea why I am here. I know nothing about mysteries. I wouldn't know a clue if it hit me in the face. But I think I am here because I don't have anything better to do. I'm in an in-between stage. I've never had money before, and I'm not sure I like how it's changing my life. On the other hand, it sure is nice. I guess until I get used to it, I'll just play amateur detective. I'm in a transition stage, my old life versus new opportunities. I'll let you know how it comes out when the paperback is published." I grinned at my reading fool of a friend. But she was in too serious of a mood for light humor.

"We're on top of a very big story, Honey."

"Practice calling me Lydia, *Mom.*"

I *know* that The Bargello is in Italy. Even *Janie* knows The Bargello is in Italy. Obviously, Marcie knew of one in Greece. Which is a tacky way of saying Corinthian columns do not a villa make. Since I was the one who drove the last leg of the trip, I pulled the van over to the side of the road of the Greek Revival entrance to The Bargello, and Janie and I sat there in awe.

She broke the silence by saying, "Doric would have made it easier to accept."

"I don't think we're gonna see Donatello's *David* here, Janie."

"Zeus, maybe."

"At least."

"Drive on," she commanded. "We've come this far. Oh, my, I just thought of something. Do you think there will be togas?"

"Hmmm, do you remember that The Bargello was once used as a prison?"

This I have to give Marcie: all tackiness aside, we were welcomed at The Bargello like long-lost relatives. Rich relatives, to be sure, but that didn't lessen the hospitality and pleasant humor of the uniformed greeters at the main entrance of the spa.

"Mrs. Bridges, welcome to The Bargello. And this must be Lydia. We've all looked forward to meeting you. And where is that scamp, Bailey? The kennel staff is so excited he's joining us."

"And he's so happy to be here," I said as I watched a swarm of attendants take my keys, my luggage, and my dog. "He's already done his business," I added as one Roman-clad attendant led Bailey to the area where the sign announced Pet Haven. "I think he's ready for a power lunch, though," I continued.

Babbling. That's what I did as the van was driven away, bags were whisked away, and Bailey led, slobbering as usual, toward another sign that announced Doggie Spa. I felt I had to babble to cover the dumbfounded look on Janie's face. That's the problem with fantasies, I thought. When you are faced with the reality of the situation, sometimes the scripted words won't come out. She got great marks with theories but failed to comprehend that when the wheels hit the dirt, the plane has gotta fly. Somehow that sounded wrong, but bottom line, I remembered how Janie actually reacted when she was in the middle of a crime scene: She melted like butter.

"Mother, are you all right?" I asked, going over to where she stubbornly held on to her backpack full of contraband junk food.

"Honey, this isn't quite like I imagined it would be."

For not the first time in my life, I thought of how my name sounding like an endearment was convenient. Even if she forgot I was Lydia, it would be okay.

We marched behind the lute and flute players as they escorted us to our rooms.

I whispered in her ear as I dragged her along the walkway with me, "We're not in Kansas anymore, Dorothy."

Thirty-Three

"I forgot to tell you something, Janie. Something that Kantor wrote." I huffed and I puffed as I remembered what Kantor had written in his letter. It's not easy to talk when you're doing rocking horses in the pool. We weren't in the deep end, the water was only bosom high, but it was hard to keep bal ance even in that depth, especially when you're only five foot one. And it also depends on the height of your bosom.

The best arena to gauge bosom size of our fellow mother/daughters was the Olympic-sized swimming pool where we did our daily water aerobics. The

Bargello furnished everyone with bathing suits, and while they weren't exactly one-size-fits-all, there was still a very ambiguous fit. Mine kept falling off at the shoulders while my new best friend Minnie's suit screamed with the effort of trying to cover her ample chest. It was Minnie doing her rocking horses beside me that kept swamping me, pulling me under water, and turning me into the picture of the famed drowned rat.

Janie waited until we had switched the set to frog leaps before she asked, "What did Kantor say? Or do I have to give you artificial respiration before you answer?" *Cute remark from someone who didn't put her heart and soul into the leaps.* How she could ignore the instructor's cries of "Harder, ladies. Harder. Put some feeling into it" was beyond me. I always thought the teacher—who stood on dry land—was talking directly to me, and I doubled my efforts until I swirled as much splash as Minnie. Then I would look over at Janie, who was smiling absently as she gently moved her arms and legs through the water.

I stopped in mid-leap; lived through the resulting wave that swept over me, and sputtered, "Honestly, Janie. You might as well have stayed in bed."

"What did Kantor say?"

"He wrote that Ms. Potter was coming to the Hill

Country this week to give him computer lessons.''

"But he hates computers.''

Janie switched to jogging in place with the rest of the group while I stood at her side. It's easy to talk in the pool. In fact, that's what most of the guests did—shouting gossip to one another—while the drill instructor raged on and on. "Right, but he likes Ms. Potter.''

Janie grinned. "Do I sense another romance in the air? Has Evelyn given up on Steven Bondesky?''

"If Kantor is buying a computer, there's something in the air. My guess is that he's planning on pumping her for information about Clover Medlock. I think he wants to break the story about Twyman and his books. The fact that Twyman didn't write them. And we all know that Ms. Potter is jealous of Clover. Imagine Bondesky as a love object!''

"Speaking of the devil," said Janie. "I've just seen her on television, but look over there, will you?''

I stopped in midstream to follow her gaze. Walking around the edge of the pool, her rubber pool shoes giving her a shuffling look, was Clover Medlock following a loquacious Marcie. Both, clad in plush white Bargello terry robes, were deep in conversation, ignoring the storm-tossed waters of the water aerobics class. However, instinct made me duck underwater as Clover suddenly turned her head toward the activity in the water.

Did I imagine it, or was there recognition in that fleeting eye contact with Clover as she watched me emerge for air?

I couldn't tell because she turned away just as quickly and continued her conversation with Marcie. They were headed for the serious swimmers' lane of the pool, separated from ours by long bobbing lengths of oval buoys.

"Do you think she saw me?" I asked Janie.

"Your own mother wouldn't recognize you. You look like a terrier caught out in the rain."

"You *are* my mother," I reminded her.

"Well, I don't know you. And the water has darkened your lighthouse red hair."

"Still," I insisted, "I thought I saw some recognition . . ."

"The big question, Honey, is what is she doing here? I thought the meeting with Gabriella, et al., was on Saturday."

The golden oldies tape that we water danced to switched to Handel, the signal that the session was over. Or it would be over following a slow, ethereal cooldown that concluded in the participants giving themselves a wet hug and then a drippy round of applause in appreciation to the instructor who hadn't dampened her wetsuit.

Minnie stood by my elbow. "Will you help me out, Lydia?"

"We'll do it together, Minnie. Inch by inch."

No one had told us our first time in the water, that leaving the pool was like reentry from outer space. The gravitational pull of weight on our bodies, which had been buoyant for the last hour, was suddenly unbearable, and my 120 pounds made me feel as heavy climbing the pool steps as Minnie's three hundred. Exiting the pool the first time had equalized us all. It was easier for me now; I didn't feel as leadened, but Minnie still suffered. Holding her by the elbow and hiding behind her was the perfect way to avoid Clover spotting me as I left the pool. As was the terry robe with the monk's hood that I slipped into as soon as I reached it at poolside. Unlike the bathing suits, the robes were not part of the package and were on sale at the gift counter—a misleading name if I ever heard one—for only $295. I had already bought three.

Minnie thanked me, and I let her go first into the showers while I stood and watched Clover taking sure, swift strokes through the water. She outdistanced Marcie by several lengths, much to the frustration of the spa owner, who obviously was still trying to impart something important to Clover.

Silently, I agreed with Janie. Clover, by my calculations, wasn't due until Saturday. What was she doing at The Bargello on Wednesday? A further question nagged me. If Clover was already here, did that mean the others were, too? Babe and Gabriella. Had Steven Hyatt gotten the dates wrong?

Thirty-Four

I met Minnie and her mom when we attended the group orientation cocktail party on Monday evening following our morning arrival. By that time, Janie and I had been measured, weighed, and assessed. Special dietary needs had been discussed . . . and no, they seriously told Janie, Twinkies did not figure in the plan. Calorie counts had been recommended. I was given the whole 1,500, and Janie received the 1,200 menu, but I knew one of the Snickers Janie had squirreled away in her backpack would put us on an even calorie count.

They kidded Janie about her daughter's red hair,

joking about the postman or the milkman, while we slipped in and out of the androgynous white robes for the data gathering. The dietitian was especially attentive to Janie, who was concerned primarily about food. That was *before* she knew about the required exercise classes. "We need to know about your allergies and your preferences," the dietitian told us.

Janie was fascinated by the shorthand on the lists, similar to the style she used in her investigation book, that the dietitian used to record our information. "What is this *recommend feathers only?* Wait, let me see that. *Allergic to fins. Hoofs ok?* I got it. That's my profile. You're saying I should only eat chicken, but beef is okay, and you have noted my fish allergy."

Now, I know Janie is not allergic to fish. I've seen her put away too many fried catfish dinners. But she was so afraid she would be on an almondine diet while she was at The Bargello that she took liberties with her profile.

It didn't take a rocket scientist to figure out that Minnie Hudson was on the 1,000-calorie-count diet list. In fact, she was joking about it when the *daughters* were separated from the *mothers* for a precounseling session. "Don't you just love it?" she had asked of no one in particular when we met in a big

Doric-columned room on the east side of the spa. "They honestly think we're gonna stick to that diet. I never have before, but they never give up on me."

"You've been here before?" I questioned her.

"Oh, yeah. Mom comes a lot, but I only come during mother/daughter weeks. She always signs us up for them and, what the heck, it's the only time we seem to get together. This your first time? I can give you all the skinny, pardon the pun, on the week. Like how to get chocolate cake out of the kitchen or seconds of potatoes."

"I think Janie—I call my mother Janie—has already covered the food angle." I laughed.

Minnie was the world's stereotype of the beautiful large woman with the jolly personality and gorgeous face. Her blond shag haircut swung easily around her face, and she seemed very comfortable with her weight and height, her almost six feet towering over me. Eyes as blue as Janie's smiled guilelessly upon the crowd of robed daughters as the first motivational speaker began her talk. She grabbed my arm and led me to a chair in the back. When Minnie led, you followed.

She whispered in my ear as we laughed at the counselor's introductory jokes about mothers and daughters and the eternal desire of mothers to know that their daughters were well-fed, meaning, of

course, that they were good mothers. "Honestly,
Lydia, if I lost weight, I'd be out of a job."

"How so?" I whispered back, thinking of cir-
cuses and sideshows.

"I'm a model for large lady catalogs. Now, don't
get me wrong, I like to stay in shape, but hey, big
is me. Wouldn't your weight look stupid on me?"

I looked at her again. She was right. A skinny
Minnie—oh my, and I thought Honey was an awful
name—would not have fit the self-assured young
woman beside me. "So I come to the sessions and
Mom and I have some laughs. And I remember
some of the good habits I always forget when I drive
out the driveway here."

Knowing someone who had been at the spa before
appealed to me; she was bound to know her way
around the buildings. "Hey, maybe you can show
me around later?"

"Sure," she agreed as we moved to another area
of the room to begin a craft project.

There was lots of laughter as twenty women of
all ages and sizes began pulling together bits and
pieces from the imaginative selections on the tables
to create a symbol of their respective mothers or
daughters. I was at a loss until I watched Minnie
wrap dozens of Three Musketeer bars in a red cel-

lophane paper and tie it with a big purple bow. "Three Ms are Mom's favorite candy. Don't worry, though, they only use Styrofoam bars under the wrappings. Too many women ate their symbols."

Carefully, I perused the tables and finally selected a silver Mylar balloon, which I surrounded with the fresh cornflowers and daisies I found in a bucket. I tied them all together at the base of the balloon with a huge bow, the same color as the cornflowers and Janie's eyes. Not satisfied, I added streamers of blue satin ribbons. Finished, I stood back to admire my creation and the helium-filled balloon headed straight toward the top of the pseudo Greek columns. It would have made it, too, except for Minnie's long reach. She grabbed it and handed it back to me. "Hey, that's pretty. Hold on tight, or it will reach the rafters."

I think I had chosen Janie's symbol well.

As had she mine.

We laughed as we exchanged the symbols in the comfortable auditorium where we all met together again. Janie had *caught* me in a candy cane Styrofoam shape wrapped with pink and green satin ribbons, the same shades as the Laura Ashley collection she had helped me pick out for my bedroom. Tied to the crooked end of the cane were streamers of dainty satin ribbons in all colors, each ribbon sporting a gold star, and the whole cane shimmered with gold glitter that glistened and flew in all directions with each movement of the cane.

"Guess I got a little carried away with the glitter." Janie grinned as she handed me my symbol.

"This is how you see me?" I asked, awed at her gift.

"This is how you see me?" she echoed as I handed her the balloon. "And of course that's you. You're my support system."

I can see why The Bargello used this opening exercise. Tears came to both our eyes as we clutched the tangible symbols of our affection.

Similar laughter and sniffling was heard throughout the auditorium as mothers and daughters saw each other through the other's eyes. Minnie held one long-stemmed yellow rose and cried, "Aw, Mom. You did it to me again."

We were so caught up in the moment, we almost missed the introduction of our hostess, Marcie Coleman, Twyman's third wife and the real reason why Janie and I were at The Bargello.

Over the roar of the excited women, I heard Janie say, "She's fat. Marcie Coleman is fat!"

"Hush, Janie, or I'll burst your balloon."

"But, Honey, she's the Martha Stewart of weight

loss. How come she gets to be fat and I have to diet?''

I jabbed her with my elbow as we sat down from the standing ovation for Marcie Coleman and repeated, ''Hush.''

One of the reasons Marcie had become such a national and international success was evident as she went directly to the issue. ''Now, I know all of you are wondering what on earth I'm doing up here— big as the side of a barn--telling all of you about weight loss and nutrition. Ladies, trust me. No one works harder to lose weight and stay in shape than I do. What is a struggle for you is a struggle for me, too. We are all in this together.''

Another roar of approval from the ladies.

Marcie didn't actually tear up, as far as I could tell, but there was a definite catch in her voice as she went on. ''Most of you know that my ex-husband, the author Twyman Towerie, died recently. I do what you do in times of stress. I eat. And eat. And eat.'' This time, the audience was silent as they didn't know whether to laugh or not. ''So, I am a bit over my goal weight right now. I know you understand that. I'll be just fine when I lose those stubborn extra ten pounds.''

This last statement finally brought a laugh from

the participants, but Janie snorted and whispered
(thank God), ''More like forty, if you ask me.''

It *was* a shock that Marcie was so large. I tried
to recall what she had looked like on the CBS special on Twyman and thought I remembered that the
clips of her had been old ones; the actual statement
about her reaction to Twyman's death had been
given by a Bargello spokesperson. I remembered
that she had a sweet face, but her blond hair in the
television special had given way to a mousy brown
color. Maybe when she gained all that weight, she
didn't feel she deserved to be blond anymore.

Marcie continued, ''When I first saw Twyman, it
was on *The Larry King Show*. I was so horrified by
his obviously deteriorating physical condition that I
called in right then and offered my services to help
him. Bless his heart, he accepted on the spot. He
came to The Bargello the next day, and we gave
him the time and privacy he needed to recoup his
health. We gave special attention to his dietary
needs because of his diabetes. Twyman and I fell in
love during the personal motivational sessions and
married right here in the garden at The Bargello.

''Our life together was wonderful. He wrote, and
I monitored every bite that went in his mouth.''

I thought she seemed a bit defensive when she
said the words *he wrote,* but then since I knew

he couldn't write his way out of a hat box, maybe I was listening for nuances that weren't there.

"Sounds like a prison to me," said Janie into my ear.

"Well, this *is* The Bargello," I answered softly.

"Unfortunately, when Twyman reentered the real world, we grew apart," said Marcie.

"And grew and grew and grew," snickered Janie.

"Although we were not one in marriage any longer, our relationship was a kind, loving, and caring one, right to the end." And Marcie stopped to sniff back a tear. The ladies in the auditorium sniffed right along with her.

"Wonder if she will admit she served him his last meal." I could not get Janie to shut up.

"I am now writing a book about my relationship with Twyman, his health needs, and our treatment of him. It will soon be available in bookstores everywhere and certainly here in our gift shop where you can also find all of my other books on diet, nutrition, and weight loss."

There was more after that commercial, but she ended with, "So you will see me this week, swimming and working out right beside you as I regain my spiritual and physical strength through diet and exercise. To your health and to mine, ladies," and there was another resounding standing ovation of cheers and applause as Marcie drifted off stage, her blue chiffon toga billowing in her wake.

"I'm going back to my room and have a Hershey bar," said Janie.

Thirty-Five

Despite her declaration to work out side by side with the other women, I didn't see Marcie Coleman at The Bargello again until she showed up at the pool with Clover on Wednesday. The spa is a large, rambling building, or rather, a series of buildings, built in a remote section of the piney woods of east Texas, so Marcie could have been there and our paths just didn't cross.

By Wednesday, Janie and I were used to the routine; breakfast in the huge canopied beds with the slippery satin comforters; facials by appointment; delicate lunches and hearty massages every after-

noon. Dinner was a dressy affair with all the participants; a time to show off the new hairstyle or
makeup that had been on the schedule for the day.

Although we had giggled over the bidets and Ja-
cuzzis in our bathrooms, Janie and I found we
quickly adapted to the luxurious life. Or, as Janie
said, "I could get used to being rich."

Much of the talk in the beauty shop and in the
dining room centered around money and how each
came to have some.

Janie boasted that our wealth came from publishing; a far cry from the actual converted gas station
she had made into a bookstore and my job as a book
rep, but the women nodded understandingly and
said theirs was from oil, of course, and *family*
money or Fortune 500 companies.

The second topic of conversation was where they
spent their money with travel being the number-one
money pit. When asked where we had traveled,
Janie replied, "Oh, lord, where have we *not* been?"
Although I could have responded with "Nowhere,"
the ladies seemed to interpret the question as answered and accepted us as equal world travelers. I
was learning that to some, sometimes it's what you
don't say that is important.

Following the water aerobics on Wednesday, we
changed our schedule to include deep heat and oil

treatments for our hair that meant heads wrapped in towels for the rest of the day and dinner in our rooms.

"A perfect time to snoop around," I told Janie.

"Okay, I'm ready for action. I'm beginning to feel like a hothouse flower." She had already put on the silk Bargello version of a sweatsuit and crept out into the dimmed corridors to case the joint before I had even returned to my adjoining room.

My plan included a prearranged meeting with Minnie, who was going to show me the staff area and hopefully Marcie Coleman's office. I shucked my white robe and was pulling the elastic waistband of the sweatpants over my hips when she knocked softly at my door.

"I'm almost ready," I told her as I opened the door and came face to face with Clover Medlock.

"Why do you insist Twyman was murdered?" she asked as she charged into the room with the west Texas stride I remembered so well.

I glanced quickly down the empty hall and closed the door. "You *did* recognize me."

"Of course. Even wet, no one else has that pinkish orange colored hair."

"Did you tell Marcie I was here?"

"Not yet. Now, answer my question about Twyman."

"That's fair," I said. "Remember, I was there when he died."

Clover sat down on the edge of the flowered chaise longue and I sat on the edge of my bed, trying not to slide off the slippery cover. I hadn't quite mastered that part of being rich.

"Right," she said, "and you saw something. Something that made you think it wasn't a natural death? I want to know what that was."

I paused, thinking how to word my next statement. "Clover, it wasn't anything I could go to the police with. Not anything tangible. If Twyman hadn't asked me how to help him with someone who was trying to kill him, it probably would never have occurred to me."

"But?"

"But, yes, he didn't do it right, the dying part, I mean."

"Pardon me? He didn't *die* right?"

"I know I haven't told you this before, but a little over ten years ago, my father died at the table. Just put his head down—it was the day after my mother had died—and he died. Now *that* was a natural death. Twyman's was . . . different."

"That's it? That's all you've been going on? A feeling?"

"Well, it's hard to explain."

"Oh, try. There has to be more to it than that for you to run all over the country interviewing starlets and visiting spas. Is this some groupie thing I don't know about, or do you genuinely think that my ex-husband was murdered? Am I a suspect, too? Don't answer that. I think I know the answer."

"I'm sorry," I said. "But you did take the blood samples."

Clover looked astonished. "How on earth do you know about that? I guess the police department has more leaks than the reporters said Ken Starr's investigation did. Did the police tell you I had taken the vials?"

"Not exactly. It was more that they *didn't* tell me that you had taken them, which made me realize— you really did. I mean, if you hadn't taken them, they would have just said so, but instead, they wouldn't answer, so I knew," I said, explaining my logic but not mentioning Silas Sampson by name. "I'm learning that what people don't tell you is sometimes more important than what they do."

Clover wasn't in any mood for my convoluted logic. She had an agenda of her own. "Well, I did take them," she confessed.

"May I ask why?"

"It was after we scattered Twyman in the stream. Up to then, I thought it was just his reckless lifestyle that had caught up with him. His time to go, you know? Then you came to the ranch and asked me if I knew who might want to kill him.'' She sighed and looked old and tired as she leaned back against the chaise cushions. New wrinkles had crept around her eyes. ''I've got to tell you, that got me to thinking. So, yeah, I took the blood samples. Hell, it's my hospital wing, I can take them if I want to.''

That's another thing I've noticed about the rich: the assumed privileges.

''What did you do with the samples? And why did you take them in the first place?''

She snorted the snort I wished I could do. ''Told the police I took them so I could spread them with his ashes. Can you believe they bought that one? Thought I was just a grief-stricken, crazy old rich lady. I really took them to have them analyzed without going through the police bullshit.''

''And did you?''

''Yep.''

''And?''

''Strange stuff in his blood. Don't know if one or the other would have killed him, but the combination . . . Have you ever heard of propranolol or metoclopramide?''

''No. What are they?'' I knew that Clover knew her drugs; knowledge acquired after years of doc-

toring sick cows and keeping the sound ones
healthy.

"From what I have found out, propranolol is a
beta-blocker and metoclopramide is a cancer drug."

"Did Twyman have cancer?" I asked.

"No, but I know who does," she answered without telling me who it was.

"Go on," I urged. "Who is it?"

"I still don't have any proof of who did it, so I
hate to say," she said. "And his blood sugar count
was way out of line."

I rearranged the towel that was slipping off my
oiled head and said, "But at least we know you
didn't do it."

Clover surprised me by saying, "I'm not so sure
about that. Oh, don't look that way. I didn't actually
murder him, but I think I started the whole thing
rolling."

"With the memoirs, you mean? You think one of
the exes did it? That's why you're here to meet with
them this Saturday?"

"Saturday?" she asked.

Before I could explain how Steven Hyatt had seen
the date in Gabriella's office, Clover looked at my
hand arranging the towel and said, "Aw, you're
wearing the ring. I'm glad."

Janie and I had decided that the diamond Twyman

had bought for Clover was part of our facade in the
world of the rich and famous, so I had reluctantly
worn it to The Bargello, grimacing every time Janie
explained about my engagement to Harry in London. She had made Harry into an earl or a count or
something. I took the ring off and offered it to Clover. "I really wish you would take it."

She was repeating what she had said at the im-
promptu streamside service for Twyman, telling me
that she wanted me to have the ring, when a knock
at the door interrupted her.

This time it really was Minnie.

"Ready for an adventure?" my new friend asked
as I opened the door. "Oh, I'm sorry, I didn't know
you had company."

"I'm just leaving," Clover said as she heaved her
way off the chaise lounge.

"No, don't go," I protested. "I can meet with
Minnie later." I didn't even bother with introductions. "I want to hear the rest of your story."

Clover patted me on the shoulder. "It will keep,
Honey. And anyway, it's almost over." She nodded
to Minnie as she went into the hall. "I really do like
you, Honey. Keep safe."

My nod to Minnie told her I would be right back,
and I chased Clover down the carpeted hall. "Clo-

ver, one more thing. You won't tell Marcie about me, will you?''

"No," she said. "This is just between me and the girls now." She cautiously looked around before pulling the white hood further over her head and scurrying off.

Thirty-Six

Minnie and I went out to check on Bailey in his canine version of spa luxury sans the bidet, but with his own huge meadow tucked away in the pines. We took him for a romp among the ubiquitous yellow wildflowers that grace Texas in the summer, and we both agreed it felt good to breathe fresh, albeit humid, air.

When I had first checked on Bailey the Monday evening we had arrived, he had been one sad dog, but since then, although he was always eager to see me, he had settled down. And, I didn't hear his howls follow me as I went back to the main building.

Minnie laughed when I told her about the dog's change in attitude. "Guess The Bargello gives new meaning to the phrase *it's a dog's life.*"

"Either that or he likes his new clothes," I agreed pointing to the bright blue bandanna tied around his neck. "He is now on a special diet. Has had two . . . make that three . . . obedience sessions. No, don't laugh. I'm trying to remember what else the vet told me. Oh, yeah. A hair and skin conditioner bath, toenails manicured, teeth brushed, and something else. Oh, I forget, but he's certainly getting *my* money's worth of attention."

"I'm sorry I interrupted you and your friend, Lydia. I wouldn't have minded waiting," Minnie apologized again.

"For the last time, silly, its okay. I'll catch up with her later. But how did you know she's my friend?"

"She kept calling you honey."

"Right," I remembered. "People call me that a lot. Reckon it has something to do with my red hair?"

"Which reminds me, I liked it straightened."

"Yeah? I think it's not really me. Wonder what they will do with it after this oil treatment."

We rambled on across the field, aimlessly following wherever Bailey's nose took him, talking for real the imagined girl talk I always thought I would have with a friend my age. I liked it.

When I arrived back at my room, Janie was waiting for me. "Don't know that I have much to add to the notebook," she confessed. "I spent most of my time in the kitchen."

"Well, get out your pen, I have *mucho* to tell," I said and told her about Clover's visit to my room.

"Wow," Janie said when I finished. "Guess that makes my Marcie and Twyman news look like second-rate stuff."

I took the notebook from her. "What is *grazer?*" I asked.

She blushed and said, "Oh, no. Not that page. That's for my Bargello notes. That's what they call someone who is a vegetarian. Don't you love it? Look at the next page."

"MRC. All is not what it seems. What does that mean?"

"Means the story she put out about Twyman, the one she told Elaine Madison, was not actually true. Marcie and Twyman *had* remained friendly. At least he thought so. She talked to him constantly by phone and fax about his diet and exercise and other health stuff. But the kitchen staff knew Marcie really hated him for leaving her for Babe. That's when Marcie got so fat.''

"You did find out some things, Janie. Why do you feel so guilty? This information kind of fits in with what Clover told me.''

"Maybe it was because it took three pieces of chocolate cake before I finished interviewing the staff. There was this shift change . . . and, well, I was hungry.''

I read on in the notebook. "Why do you have the word *Babe* with a question mark?''

She was excited as she remembered and told me, "Yes, yes. Babe. Although Marcie hates Babe, talks ugly about her all the time, she had started talking to her on the phone a lot. Something about a special diet. The chef thinks Babe might be sick.''

"Tired maybe. Babe looked exhausted when I saw her in Vegas, but I don't think sick." I yawned and complained, "I'm really tired of this towel around my head, but the plastic cap looks awful by itself. Is your head beginning to itch?''

"Take a nap. You have time before they deliver dinner.''

"I think I will. I'm glad we don't have to go to the dining room for dinner tonight. And I guess you'll be too full to eat what they deliver.''

"I reckon *not*. Wait till you see what they are

fixing for us. I watched them make up the supper. Oh, and the staff made me take this bottle of wine to go with it."

I fell asleep on the satin comforter while Janie related The Bargello box supper menu.

Thirty-Seven

Reckon the unaccustomed schedule of exercise and massages plus the strain of living a lie finally clicked in. It was like, *Hello, body to Honey. You will sleep now. Sleep right through the most expensive box supper you never ate in your life. Sleep right through a bottle of contraband wine and your play-pretend mother's attempts to wake you and share it with her. Sleep. Sleep.*

When I awoke, it was dark, and I was disoriented and thirsty. I longed to tear the plastic cap off my head and wash the oil treatment out of my hair, but I didn't seem to have the energy to move. Flashbacks of the vivid dream that had finally awakened me kept interfering with my ability to think and move. Finally, I literally rolled off the bed onto the floor and crawled to the mini-fridge in my room. I gulped one of the bottles of orange juice. Eventually, visions of cows with sick eyes faded from my thoughts, and I rose and staggered into the bathroom.

The hot shower revived me further, and the vigorous towel drying I gave my hair finished the job. Looking in the mirror, I saw that my hair had stubbornly returned to its natural curly state, although it now felt soft and silky as I ran my fingers through the drying strands. Suddenly the warm, steamy air of the bathroom made me feel claustrophobic. I longed for fresh air.

The wide, carpeted hallways were dim and silent as I padded barefoot down the hallway, The Bargello robe covering my body and head.

Vaguely, I thought of finding the twenty-four–hour gift shop where guests were encouraged to use the honor system in purchasing gifts and health-related items in addition to a full Bargello designer wardrobe.

A customer would just take what they wanted and fill in a sales slip on one of the dozens of clipboards on the counter. You marked the items you had picked out and signed your name. No hassle of dealing with nasty money or plastic credit cards. The daytime clerk collected the slips from the bright yellow plastic box and graciously added them to your bill. Somehow it made all the merchandise seem free, so you just bought and bought and bought. Which, of course, was the idea. I had noticed that security cameras in the store backed up the honor system, though.

What I had in mind was a book I had seen when Minnie and I had browsed the stock earlier in the day. No, that was yesterday, I remembered, as I glided noiselessly down the hall. I don't know why people call two A.M. the middle of the night when it's really the beginning of the day.

I knew just where the book was, visualizing it in my mind, as I turned left at the second hallway. It was nestled beside Marcie's extensive inventory of health, diet, exercise, and Bargello cookbooks. Marcie had not written this book, but she had written the forward to it, a glossary of interactive drugs. I wanted to look up the drugs Clover had told me were found in Twyman's blood samples.

This thought and the ironic notion that although Marcie was the only wife who Twyman hadn't stolen a book from while he was married to her occupied my mind to the extent that I suddenly realized I was lost in the maze of halls. I found myself at what I remembered to be the door to the kennel. *Marcie couldn't write. Oh, she has all those books with her name on them, but the woman can't write. No wonder Twyman had left her for Babe. Nothing to steal.*

I decided to give Bailey a beginning-of-morning hug before I retraced my steps to the gift shop.

I was bending over his cage, trying to figure out how to get the wire door open, when someone came up behind me and grabbed me around the waist. A man's hand covered my mouth. The hand stifled my instinctive scream, and I struggled to get away.

"Georgie Porgie, pudding and pie."

I bit the hand before the words sank in.

"Ouch."

I almost sobbed. "Kissed the girls and made them cry?"

"When the boys came out to play," came the pained response.

"Georgie Porgie ran . . . Oh, Steven, you scared me to death. What on earth are you doing here?" I turned in his arms and gave him the two-fisted beating that I had been going to give an unknown assailant.

"Whoa. That's enough. Ouch. Stop that, Honey. And here I thought you needed protection. *Wrong!*"

We collapsed on the ground before Bailey's cage.

"Nice robe. Makes you look like a ghostly nun."

I wrapped the now-open robe around the long, pastel Bargello sleep shirt I wore. "I'm glad you like it. I bought you one. Can you let Bailey out? He thinks we're playing."

"Yeah? What game?" He reached over and twisted the plastic lock on the cage. Bailey bounded out and licked us both enthusiastically.

Suddenly suspicious, I asked, "Steven, how long have you been here? I thought you were going to Hollywood."

Steven Hyatt stretched his lanky length on the grass while Bailey scampered around, visiting friends in the other cages. He seemed to be taunting them with, *Hee hee, I'm out and you're not.*

"I came Monday night. Hey, I work here."

"Oh, right. Doing what? No, don't tell me. You're the new masseuse they were telling me about?"

He straightened up with dignity. "I'll have you know I am the official Bargello dog walker and night guard."

I rolled on the grass, choking with laughter. "Won't let you near the women, eh? Good instincts."

"Not until they finish my security check, but what the hey, a job's a job."

"Obviously you've come here to guard and protect Janie and me. Ah, Steven, did you think there would be trouble in spa city?"

"Now where would our Nancy be without her Ned?"

I hadn't realized I had missed Steven so much. It had only been four days, but it felt good to be bantering with him as we lay in the grass, accepting quick licks from Bailey as he enjoyed his unexpected freedom.

"*That's* why Bailey settled down. He didn't pine for me because he had his own playmate and constant companion. Now tell me why you didn't go to Hollywood, and just maybe I'll tell you all Janie and I have learned about Twyman."

Steven told me that after thinking about all his and Silas's jokes about us being safe at a ladies' spa, he had remembered I could get in deadly trouble right in my own house. So he had put his Hollywood trip on hold for a week and come to east Texas to stand guard. He'd found an immediate opening in the kennel, but his security clearance had left him frustrated. Until they had further checked his background and references, he wasn't allowed near the main buildings. "I sleep right here with the dogs," he said, and his nod indicated a cement blockhouse behind him, which also stored feed and supplies for the animals.

I reached in my robe pocket and gave him a plastic keycard. "Here, I have two. I lost mine the first day and they replaced it. When I told them I'd found it under the bed, they just said they would rekey it so they both worked. Take it. You never know when it will come in handy."

"Yeah, like maybe I could slip into your room and we could . . ."

Steven gave me a demonstration of what we might do if he came to my room, and I was very surprised at my reaction. Somehow, in all the years I had known him, this view of Steven Hyatt had never crossed my mind. It felt good, I thought, to be held and caressed by him. I snuggled against his neck. "Hmmm, you smell like wet dog."

He sighed. "So much for romance. Okay, you're dying to tell me. What have you and Janie discovered that is more important than this?" And he gave me a very nice kiss.

"Janie who? Oh, you mean *Mother?*" I pulled my robe together again and sat with my knees tucked under my chin, my arms wrapped around my legs. Hot as it was in east Texas in August, it was chilly and damp on the grass at two in the morning.

I told Steven about Clover visiting my room, about what Janie had found out about Marcie and Babe from the kitchen staff. Finally, I asked him if he could have gotten the dates wrong in Gabriella's office.

"No, it said Saturday, August the eighth. Why?"

"Because Clover seemed confused when I said I knew they were all meeting on Saturday. Like I had gotten the date wrong."

"Did it ever occur to you, maybe they changed the date?"

Thirty-Eight

"Of course," said Janie when we shared our breakfasts-in-bed on the floor of my room the next morning. "That must be it. Anyway, I can find out easily enough. Karen in the front office is the sous-chef's sister. You wouldn't believe what trouble she is going through with her husband. Her sister is just beside herself with worry. I swear half the world is having marital problems."

"That I believe," I agreed. "I hope you don't take this personal, Janie, but the last happily married couple I knew died when my mother and father died."

"Were they really happy, Honey? Or is that just how you remember it?"

I looked at her. "Good question, Janie. Devoted, certainly. Loyal, absolutely. Happy? Yes, I'm sure they were."

"Are you going to eat that other piece of English muffin?"

I passed her the muffin and said, "Find out from the receptionist Karen when Babe and Gabriella are coming. But be careful. Remember, if we are right about Twyman, and it's looking more and more like we are, one of them is a murderer."

"Just one of them? Sounds to me like we're looking at a *Murder on the Orient Express* situation. I think they all did him in. And as far as me being in danger, what about you? You run around in the middle of the night and you worry about *me?* Tell me some more about Steven Hyatt. Did he propose again?"

"He mentioned something about it, yes."

"Lord, Honey, you're blushing. So, what did you tell him this time?"

"Same thing. That I don't know. I don't know. I don't know. What I do know is that I have to see Harry first. I made up my mind about that. Soon as we leave here, I'm going to get a passport and go to London and find him."

She thought about it as she chewed my muffin. "That works. I understand that. If I didn't have to find a lawyer and get on with the divorce, I'd go with you." And then she laughed.

"What?"

"Lord, look at you Honey. Four months ago, you wouldn't say boo to a goose. Now you're heading overseas."

"I hate to think it's the money that makes the difference, but it certainly has changed my life," I admitted. "Which reminds me, I need to call Bondesky and make sure that the money is safe."

She reassured me, "Oh, I'm sure it is. I'd put my money on Bondesky."

I reminded her, "I did."

In the end, we didn't need Karen's confirmation that Babe was arriving early at The Bargello. By the time I reached the facial room, every woman at the spa was talking about the star's early-morning arrival. I listened as the attendant deep-cleansed my face and neck with cool lotions and soothing creams that she rhythmically applied with soft, warm sponges.

"I heard that Marcie met her personally at the door. Babe flew into Dallas and a limousine brought her straight here."

"I heard that there is a man with her. Wonder where they will put him?"

"Who is he? And I'm sure she's going into the private wing. They have suites over there."

"I heard that she is sick. Now, don't go telling this, but I mean *really* sick."

"I think he's her manager or something like that."

"Don't you think it's strange that Babe and Marcie are friends? I mean, after all, Twyman Towerie left Marcie to marry Babe."

"Isn't that just like a man? Did I tell you about my second husband?"

"It was my third that gave me fits, but what can you expect from a man that you meet at a casino on the Riviera?"

"I have more food on my face right now than I have in my stomach," came a complaint from a voice beside me.

I took the cotton pads off my eyes and raised my head only to be greeted with a shot of warm mist. Before the beautician clucked at me and put the pads back on my eyes, I had made out the large form of Minnie on the table next to me. "Let me guess," I said. "Cucumber, chamomile, and a little rosemary and thyme?"

We giggled and sang an off-key version of "Scarborough Fair."

Everyone in the room laughed, but one woman said, "Oh, you young things. Just you wait. When you're our age, you'll be glad your mothers brought you here. Can't get a man with a rough complexion, you know."

I asked Minnie, but the whole room listened, "Is that what you want, Minnie? To catch a man?"

"I don't know, Lydia. I think I would like for a man to catch *me*. No, I would like for us to catch each other. I want a man who respects me as much as I respect him. Who thinks my thoughts are as important as his. That my decisions are as valid as his. One whose ego lets *me* have a life, too."

The facial room grew quiet, and we could hear the waterfall of the mood tape in the silence as the half-dozen women and their attendants thought about Minnie's words. Finally, one beautician called Minnie by my name as she said, "Get real, honey, I've worked here for over six years. I've never met a happily married woman yet."

"She's right," said one of the older women from her table. "It all stops after the wedding."

"So," asked Minnie with a chuckle in her voice, "why is it that I'm supposed to get married?"

* * *

Janie reported at lunch that Gabriella Rusi was due in at three that afternoon.

I felt goose bumps rise on my skin as I said, "This is it, then. The gathering of the *girls*. All the women who loved Twyman, married him, and kept his secret."

"Yeah," said Janie. "Wonder why they did that?"

"Reckon we're fixing to find out."

Thirty-Nine

It was easy to be flip when I was lying in the lap of luxury, getting a facial followed by a languid massage. Easy to talk about climaxes and wax eloquent on other people's relationships. Be superior about love and marriage. Smug even.

It was another thing to have both of my arms firmly secured to one of the chair arms of The Bargello conference room chairs with silver duct tape. As were my ankles to the chair's legs. Not only did I feel claustrophobic, I felt downright helpless as I watched four women finish a chapter in their lives that had begun long before I knew they were even writing it.

The only one of Twyman's ex-wives I hadn't seen personally was Gabriella Rusi, but I could have picked her out of the midway crowd in the middle of Cotton Bowl Sunday at the height of the State Fair of Texas in Dallas. Steven Hyatt's original description of the author's second wife certainly helped, as did the fact that I first saw her talking to Clover in the hallway.

I'm afraid I had been sleuthing on my own again, which should be a lesson to me, when I saw Clover hurrying down a hallway I hadn't been down before. It was the hall to the private wing and was heavily monitored with security cameras. I hadn't figured out how to snoop there without being seen, but when I saw Clover in her white robe head down that hall, I followed her. I wanted the answer to some questions.

Although the hood covered her head, I knew it was Clover. No one else walked the way she did, like she was walking the range, closing in on some prey. She disappeared around the corner of the rambling private area, the super deluxe wing where Marcie lived and it was rumored that Babe was ensconced and where I presumed Clover was lodged also.

It was late when I chased after Clover. Middle of the night late. I had actually been on my way to let Steven in the main building. I knew he had the key I had given him, but he didn't have a clue as to how to find his way around inside the spa. We had decided when I visited Bailey to meet at eleven that night at the entrance nearest the kennel where I would guide him back to my room for a conference with Janie and me. Steven wanted to call Silas Sampson back in Fort Worth and fill him in on what we had found out. I argued that we didn't have enough facts to call our favorite detective, but Steven said Clover's confession about the blood samples was enough.

Janie waited back in my room—with snacks from the kitchen—for both of us.

I was honestly going to play it out that way. Then I saw Clover scampering down the hall like the white rabbit from *Alice,* and I followed.

At the corner of the hall where I lost Clover, I hesitated before choosing a direction. Right or left? Right felt right, but since I was always wrong, I turned into the hallway on the left. Who knew that for the first time in my life I would be right the first time?

The hallway to the left was empty, but behind me, just around the corner of the right hallway, I heard voices. I turned quickly but not before the two hooded figures had seen me.

Gabriella was tall and lithe in her white robe. The hood was pulled back from her head and I was mesmerized by her startling dark good looks. I wondered why Steven had never told me how beautiful she was. Her actual beauty had never come across so dramatically on the televised segments I had seen her on, in which she just looked foreign and vaguely mysterious. In real life, maybe it was the robe; she looked like a high priestess.

"What do you want?" she demanded. "This is a private wing."

"I'm lost," I said. "I was taking this robe to a friend and turned the wrong way. It's so easy to get lost around here, you know. I am so sorry." I held up the robe that I had been taking to disguise Steven Hyatt as I spoke.

My chatty excuse might have worked if Clover hadn't blurted out my name with a gasp: "Honey!"

Gabriella glanced at Clover before returning her dark, soulful eyes back to me. "Honey? *The* Honey? The one with the fruit name? My, my."

I decided right then and there that Gabriella was the killer.

Maybe it was the gun she pulled from her robe pocket and held in my face.

Forty

I just read in *People* magazine where some famous detective said that he could always figure out the perpetrator from the clues left at the crime scene. For instance, if guns were used, the odds were super high that it was a man. I think my experience at The Bargello would definitely put a sock in his statistics.

Gabriella used hers, a Smith and Wesson twenty-five-caliber semiautomatic, to wave me into a nearby room, which turned out to be Marcie's conference room. Both Marcie and Babe were seated at the marble-topped conference table, and their mouths fell open as they saw me, but that was nothing compared to what their eyes did when they saw Gabriella with the gun.

Marcie was the first to speak. "Gabriella, don't be a fool. Put that down. This is one of the guests."

Babe said, "Oh, shit."

"Marcie, *this* is our little snoop. Meet Honey . . . What is your last name, anyway?"

"Huckleberry," said Clover. "And she's a friend of mine. Stop that, Gabriella. Put down that gun."

"No, I don't think so. Not until I'm sure our Miss Honey knows the whole story. Sit down, honey."

"Thank you, but I must be going," I said.

"I don't think so." Gabriella laughed. "Marcie, dear, get something to tie her up."

Clover snorted her dear snort. "Gabby, are you serious? This is just a child."

"Sit down, Clover. I came here to get some answers, and this child, as you call her, is part of it, so I want her to stay." Gabriella turned the gun on Marcie. "Marcie, do as I say."

A white-faced Marcie rummaged through a drawer in a side table and came up with a roll of duct tape. "Will this do?"

When I was secure to Gabriella's satisfaction but not to mine, Gabriella laid the gun on the table and said, "Okay, now everybody sit down."

It was obvious that she felt herself in charge of

the meeting. She didn't actually give the *come to order* command, but she did start the ball rolling with a jolt. "Okay. Now which one of you idiots killed Twyman?"

So I was wrong in thinking it was Gabriella who murdered Twyman, just like I was wrong in thinking Steven Bondesky had killed Steven Miller. Constrained and uncomfortable as I was, I found that I was interested in the answer, too.

There was a long pause as the other women stared at each other, each waiting for the other to go first. Finally, Clover said, "Marcie did it."

"I did not. Babe did. At least it was her idea."

"No way, Marcie," Babe retorted. The Vegas star *did* look sick. Without her stage makeup, her face was pale and translucent. She looked weak and fragile in the light of the chandelier hanging over the conference table. "I sent you those pills, yes, but you're the one who put them in Twyman's potatoes."

Marcie countered the accusation with, *"You're* the one who told me those cancer drugs would be fatal to a diabetic."

Babe had been taking lessons from Clover, but her snort was weak and lacked the importance of Clover's favorite expression of disgust. Her sarcasm meter was still running on high, though. "Especially with that incorrect dose of insulin that you gave him, Marcie. How did you talk him into letting you mix his dose? And, no, you're the one who is the expert on drug interaction. You knew my medications would be fatal to Twyman. All I did was send you a dozen of the pills.''

It was like a tennis match, with Clover, Gabriella, and me playing the parts of the fans who sit in the stands, our eyes switching back and forth to whoever was hitting the ball. Gabriella still thought she was the referee, and she stopped the play.

"You mean your cancer drugs killed Twyman?" she asked Babe.

I wish I knew when to keep my mouth shut, but I was little miss know-it-all, and answered for Babe. "I could see where they would do that. I have this friend, well, she's a client, actually, in Jacksboro. Juliana. And her aunt used to own this bookstore called Papyrus. Well, to make a long story short, the aunt died because she was a diabetic and the cancer drugs—she had cancer—worked against the insulin she took for her diabetes.''

Gabriella gave me a long silencing look before she asked Babe, "And you sent these drugs to Marcie?''

"And so Twyman died of an insulin reaction?" asked Clover.

"Shut up, Clover," said Gabriella. "If you hadn't written your memoirs, none of this would have happened in the first place."

"It was time someone called Twyman on his plagiarism," replied Clover. "I should have done it when he first claimed *For All the Wrong Reasons* was his book, not mine, but oh, no, he convinced me that the public would never accept such a book from a woman."

"The memoirs scared him," said Marcie. "It would have ruined his career."

"Well, bless his heart," said Gabriella. "And what do you think it would have done to mine?"

"You were stupid, Clover," said Babe. "And Twyman was a real jerk."

"Then why did you take him away from me?" asked Marcie.

"Now, that wasn't hard to do, was it?" Babe smirked.

"Tempers, tempers, ladies," yelled Gabriella above the accusations.

It was Clover who brought the meeting to a standstill. "What happens now?" she asked.

The collected, rejected wives of the second-bestselling author in the world all turned as one to look at me.

"I won't say a word. Honest," I told them.

"Liar, liar, pants on fire," whispered Babe.

Forty-One

It was when Gabriella picked up her gun that I finally got scared. The exotic-looking woman seemed all business, and the business she was interested in was silencing me. It dawned on me that I could die.

As it must have to Clover.

"Wait a minute, Gabby. Don't be so hasty, now." And Clover pulled a small, black two-shot Derringer from her pocket.

And Gabriella shot her.

And I wet my pants.

Marcie also had a gun in her robe pocket. She aimed a Beretta seven-shot—six in the clip and one in the pipe—at Gabriella and killed her.

"Well, shit, that about cuts it for me," said Babe as she stood and picked up Gabriella's fallen gun. She killed Marcie without blinking an eye.

I waited for the sounds of the reverberating shots to die down, but they were still echoing in my ears as Babe turned the gun on me.

"Relax, Honey," Babe reassured me. She put a strip of duct tape over my mouth. "Someone has to be around to tell the whole story. You're home free." She headed for the door. "See you in the funny papers."

It was Silas Sampson who told me who had what gun. I didn't know anything about guns before being shut up with the four angry women, but what I know now I will never forget.

It was also Silas Sampson who told Janie that forensics experts have proved that 20 percent of people do sleep through gunshots, even those that are shot in the same room with them. And for her not to be so devastated that she hadn't awakened when shot after shot careened through the conference room, waking every other guest and worker at The Bargello.

Even Steven Hyatt had heard them from outside, where he waited patiently, playing with Bailey, for me to lead him to my room. Hearing the gunfire, he used his card key to open the door and ran in to find half-naked women roaming the halls. They screamed when they saw him, certain that he was the source of the mayhem. That's why he ran down the hall shouting, "Police, police. I'm an officer."

It took them forever to find me.

By that time, I had managed to scoot the chair on its rollers over to the door and break two of my toes hammering them against the conference room door.

It was Bailey who had bounded in behind Steven, and it was Bailey who eventually guided him down the correct corridor. He found an attendant at the conference room door. "I'm looking for Marcie. She's not in her room." Then he opened the door and found her.

The worker ran to Marcie, and Steven ran to me. He ripped the silver tape from my mouth. It hurt so badly, I could hardly tell him, "I think Clover is still alive."

Steven looked around the room that smelled of gunpowder, blood, and urine, trying to identify which bloodstained white robe belonged to Clover.

"Under the table," I said, as I indicated where I had heard someone moaning while I had battered the door.

"Jesus," said the attendant as he surveyed the blood-spattered room.

The room filled with people, and I lost track of events after that.

Eventually, someone took me back to my room and awakened Janie, who had fallen asleep over a bowl of ice cream while waiting for Steven and me.

It was much later, way after one of the EMTs had bandaged my toes—I refused to go to the hospital— that Janie and I had a chance to talk. Bailey lay on the bed by my side; I had insisted that he not be returned to the kennel. Janie was aghast at my story. It was not with pride but with remembrance that she said, "I told you they all did it. Just like the *Orient Express*. I finally got one right."

It was Janie who told the bewildered Jefferson police to call Detective Silas Sampson in Fort Worth. He arrived early in the morning, only minutes after Abbie Gardenia and her camera crew. One of them I saw, the other I declined.

Forty-Two

"So who is getting the credit for actually killing Twyman?" asked Janie.

"No one. There's no proof he was murdered. Clover threw away the report on the blood samples along with the vials before she came to The Bargello. The drugs might have been in something Marcie got him to eat before the luncheon. If the cancer drug was in the potatoes, he didn't have time to eat them at lunch. Remember that I saw him eat his pie first. And no one actually saw Marcie give Twyman his insulin injection that morning. No one saw Marcie at all, but Elaine has confirmed she was there."

Janie wrinkled her nose in disgust. "So, they all get away with it?"

"Janie," I reminded her. "They're dead. I hardly call that walking off scot-free."

"Just the same . . ." she muttered.

We were at home in Fort Worth, curled up for a postmortem on the pink and green Laura Ashley quilt on my bed. Bailey stretched his long body between us, snoring soft trumpet sounds now that most of the teatime goodies had been consumed. Since the massacre at The Bargello, he hadn't wanted to get a foot away from me.

Janie sipped her hot tea gone cold and wondered, "Honey, what did Twyman mean when he asked you about someone killing him?"

"I can only imagine, Janie, but this is my guess. I think that he didn't have a clue that the wives were plotting to murder him; I think he meant if Clover published her memoirs, he would be dead professionally. To him, fame was everything. That's why he was so desperate to have Clover marry him again. That's why, when he thought I was a book detective, he imagined I could help him. To have been discovered a fraud would have *killed* his reputation, made him a laughingstock to the public, and ruined his career. He was a desperate man, asking *me* for advice."

"What an ego," she observed.

"Yep, that's what he boiled down to, a super ego with a humongous appetite."

"Speaking of . . . do you want that last croissant?"

"No, you can have it."

"Thanks, although I shouldn't. I can't believe I gained ten pounds at The Bargello. Those places aren't all they're cracked up to be, you know." She buttered the croissant as she asked, "Are you going to keep the ring?"

I looked down at the pink diamond on my finger. "I don't know. Wait. That's not true. I *am* going to keep it. Clover gave it to me, and maybe it will always remind me of something."

"Like what?"

"Hmm . . . *pride goeth before a fall?*"

"*The way to a man's heart is through his stomach?*"

I concluded, "How about always eat your vegetables first?"

Forty-Three

I walked slowly across the field with Steven Bondesky on a cloudy, damp summer morning, a week after the tragedies in east Texas. We supported each other in our hesitant progression toward our destination.

To divert his thoughts from our chore, I asked him about the investments he had made for me. His evasive answer could have been attributed to his current state of mind, so I chattered on to distract him, but privately, I wondered if anything had happened to my money. "I made a new friend at the Bargello. Her name is Minnie. She lives in New

York, and I'm going to see her there next week when I go to Steven Hyatt's movie premiere. Then, as I told you, I'll go from there to London to see what I can find out about Harry.''

The old man wasn't paying a bit of attention to me. "Where are they going to bury that movie star?''

"Her friend Kevin Richardson called me last night. He's burying her in Las Vegas. They had a home there.''

It was Kevin who had driven Babe away from The Bargello in their limousine to a prearranged destination. Babe had still been wearing her Bargello robe when the grief-stricken man had called the police to come for her body. Babe had found a Texas version of Dr. Kevorkian; she had planned her death weeks before she came to the spa. "There was no hope for her,'' Kevin told me, "and she wanted to die while she still had her dignity, before she lost all her strength and independence.''

And it was Kevin who finally answered the last question I had about Twyman Towerie. "Twyman left Clover to marry Gabriella. She was the best in the business, and he wanted her to promote his book. She didn't know until *Down by the Riverside* came out that he had stolen the manuscript from one of her clients. The son of a bitch had found it in her office; the client had died, and Gabriella's secretary couldn't find any family to return it to, and, well, somehow Twyman got hold of it and realized what a masterpiece it was. The man couldn't write, but he did know good work when he saw it. Gabriella didn't have anything to do with Twyman's death, but she wasn't unhappy that he died. It was Clover that she was afraid of. Clover's memoirs would have ruined her business; her clients would never have trusted her again.''

The sun broke out amid the clouds, reminding Bondesky and me that summer was still with us.

I said gently, ''You're Clover's executor. Are you going to publish her memoirs?''

He breathed an old man's sigh of worry and regret. ''I don't know. I honestly don't know.''

We stopped by the sassy running waters of the creek on Clover's land, the original spot where the ranch owner had first met the man who was eventually killed by the words he claimed to have written. Bondesky opened the gold urn and, with a sudden burst of strength, sprayed the contents of the vessel high into the air.

Clover's ashes flew into a high arc and then fell into the constantly running water, forming a gray comet on the silvery surface before disappearing into the stream.

I looked around. The field was empty. The girls had all gone home.

<u>Jane Waterhouse</u>

"Waterhouse has written an unusual story with plenty of plot twists. Garner Quinn is a memorable creation and the book's psychological suspense is entirely successful."
—*Chicago Tribune*

<u>GRAVEN IMAGES</u>

A murder victim is discovered, piece by piece, in the lifelike sculptures of a celebrated artist. True crime author Garner Quinn thinks she knows the killer. But the truth is stranger than fiction—when art imitates life...and death

___0-425-15673-7/$5.99

A Choice of the Literary Guild®
A Choice of the Doubleday Book Club®
A Choice of the Mystery Guild®

Prices slightly higher in Canada

A JACK FLIPPO MYSTERY

DOUG SWANSON

UMBRELLA MAN

PUTNAM